Eleanore Hill

Author of seven books that chronicle the
distance that women have traveled, from few
choices to making hard choices along the way
toward an enforced independence. Eleanore goes
well beyond coping, into creating a new life, and
then another one. Reversing roles. The life worth
living carries her personal stamp on it—that's the
message in Eleanore Hill's *Corduroy Leopard*.

Corduroy Leopard

Eleanore Hill

Gingerbread Girl Press

Carpinteria CA • 2016

Corduroy Leopard © Eleanore Hill 2016
Gingerbread Girl Press ISBN 978-0-9970495-0-3

Books by Eleanore Hill

The Family Secret

The Last American Housewife

Period Pieces

How to Cook for Your Dog

In the Aftermath of an Overdose

To Be a Landlady

The Gingerbread Girl

Corduroy Leopard

Contents

We Were the Divorcing Generation

These short retro glimpses were written between 1962 to 1982, the twenty years when women got old. They went into marriage, had babies, served a "master" in the way of a husband whom they tried to please. The home became a beautiful trap ultimately. We married in our early twenties, went into it as butterflies, and came out as caterpillars twenty years later.

We were the divorcing generation....

These short retro glimpses were written between 1962 to 1982, the twenty years when women got old. They went into marriage, had babies, served a "master" in the way of a husband whom they tried to please. The home became a beautiful trap ultimately. We married in our early twenties, went into it as butterflies, and came out as caterpillars twenty years later. We were the divorcing generation. Went into what society expected young women between the ages of 18 to 21, to do. If you didn't marry, you became an "old maid." Movies like *A Streetcar Named Desire*, showed Vivien Leigh already "over the hill" in her thirties with the likes of Marlon Brando, in his twenties, rubbing her nose in it. Just watch any of the old sepia-colored movies. Women did not go sit at sidewalk cafes and sip coffee. There weren't any back then; and a woman's place was in the home doing her housework and tending the children. We were still close to a Biblical foundation that taught paying attention to the skin was a sin, in a sense. Of course, if you look at your mother's and grandmothers' old black- and-white photos taken with a Brownie box camera, you see that they grew old as they were suppose to, once "the bloom of youth" wore off and "let nature take its course." Anyone other than professional models, movie stars or professional sex workers, had no excuse to keep looking "beautiful." Chemicals in makeup back then was a jar of Ponds face cream, or any homemade concoction made from goose grease and lye, or rose petals soaked in water, clay packs, beef steaks, chilled tea bags and the original astringent, besides splashing cold water in your face, Witch Hazel. So, the average woman was not much more than a plain-faced nun. Dolling up and going out was a rare thing for the middle class woman of those times. Most had never entered a bar, smoked a cigarette, or even drank anything but lemonade.

These stories depict the fear and ever vigilant eye of such a woman, as she sees her first crowsfoot at the corner of her eye in her late twenties, entering her thirties, tending her children and husband, who, in this case is a hard-to-please critic. As she steams up over laundry, the stove cooking dinner, her lipstick crawls up the lines forming in her upper lip, like mercury in a thermometer, she looks in the mirror and truly believes it's all over for her, being "young." Today, of course, there are no age clothes where toddlers are dressed like dolls and old women have to wear old woman clothes. The times have put grand-mothers and grandkids in the same sweats and tennis shoes. Eleanor Roosevelt died at 77, looking 100 years old. Jane Fonda, at 77, looks 16, if you don't get too close. Dyeing your hair, get-ting a nip and a tuck, liposuction, fillers and extractions, are all okay. Between 1960 and 1980, women would have been consid-ered vain, which was looked upon as fear of growing old. You were suppose to get glasses, a gut, loose flapping upper arms, false teeth, and wrinkles. Wrinkles! It was enough to scare you into obedience, so you wouldn't end up "out there" without the means to wash your face and roll your hair. Look at the boy and girl twins, the Brinkleys: Christy still looks like she did as a teen model. Her twin brother looks like someone's grandpa. Times have changed; but these stories show the astute eye of a housewife who looked for signs of aging, almost obsessively, however educated and accomplished she was and would become in her later life. She is in her 20's and 30's in these pieces.

Eleanore Hill
May 2016

1.

The Requirement: about self-consciousness over her face at 32 because she's not 22 but she's in love. The rule of the day back then was only young people deserved to fall in love. If older people did, it was a kind of joke.

The Requirement

She got to the park first and walked along to the spot where she could wait for him. Her face felt big and loose and long, dangling out where he could be watching it if he had decided to do that, to hide and watch her waiting for him. If he wanted to study her before she saw him the way she liked to study him before he saw her. After he knew that she saw him he would not look the same. And after she knew he had spotted her she would begin to perform even though she would try not to.

She sat on the lawn and then spread her sweatshirt out and lay facing the entrance and opened Down All The Days before her and tried to read. Her face hung out and she felt that it was becoming monstrous and misshapen. She had pores on her cheeks that had begun to enlarge and pucker. There were crinkles around her eyes and the fat part of her cheeks had slid down beside her mouth, the next step being for them to slide right off her jaw and hang, as they did on older women.

And because she was one step away from her cheeks sliding off her jaw as she waited, she was unable to look at her book. She wanted to spot him first so she could study him coming and beat him to studying her.

She saw a figure of a man up under the underpass and knew instantly that it was him because of the shape of the hair. She got up and started toward him not able to lie there after all and watch him coolly. Her arms felt like the loose dangling arms of a monkey as soon as she knew he spotted her and she wished she were not so awkward. When two people are in love they should be beautiful. Not just to each other, but beautiful. She could not love freely until she was. So she would not love freely.

The next day, he was sitting hunched over and red and short haired at his table, eating breakfast alone when she knocked. He hadn't gotten up to meet her at the door, but waited for her to come, listening to her approaching car, the slam of the door and her footsteps. She had done that too, many times, listened warmly to the sounds he made coming to see her. It was a kind of treat, something to savor, listening to someone coming to you.

She saw him there, sitting with his knees crossed like a woman. His shoulders were rounded and he held a fork over a bowl of eggs as if he were a portrait in still life.

He had turned and was looking at the door as she entered. He said, "You better have come, Jesus." And then he was across the room in one step, still distracted, but hugging her.

"I'm glad you came. I needed to see you. I had a bad night." He kissed her face somewhere. It was brisk and he told her he was going to make a phone call and would be right back. He was out the door, hollering back in his gentle tenor, "Have some coffee."

She poured a cup and dug into the brown sugar box for a teaspoon of granules, poured milk from the carton sitting out and then sat down in a chair opposite his at the little round table which was covered over with a square blue oil cloth. She began visualizing trimming off the pointed corners which hung down unevenly. An ashtray full of loose burnt tobacco and very little paper on the butts was next to her cup.

She picked up a copy of West and glanced through it and studied a girl in a bikini, waiting, cooling, and warming and trying to stay warm. There was a fat new pillow on one of the sofas and a flowered soft suitcase beside a chair. The phonograph was playing music, heavy music, sex music, which didn't go with the sunshine coming in the window or with the fresh air.

He came back and she had a moment of listening to his steps approach before she saw him. First he was not there and then he was there, and seeing him was like magic. Out of nothing there came a man and she loved him instantly, as soon as he appeared. He said, "It is such a treat to see you sitting there this morning. I didn't sleep well last night. And Jesus, what dreams."

He sat down again and began finishing his eating. "Why? What was wrong?" she asked watching his jaw working gently, and liking the way he looked up at her from the angle at which he hunched.

"I was really disappointed when you didn't show yesterday. I thought you would."

"My brother came," she interrupted him. "I had to pick him up at the airport about five. He's in from Africa." She wanted to cut the table cloth corners off again.

2.

Hands, The Letter, Sand All Over Them
are all about having an affair in her thirties and
not being young.

Hands

Our hands were there at the Somerset. Crawling from lap to lap to clasp one another, lifting glasses of scotch and water to lips, finding bumps on arms, faces, napkins, sides of glasses, the table top. Finding itches. Finding hair on arms and rubbing over it, pulling at it. Finding moisture and things in corners of eyes and loose skin on lips, and a green cherry in a gimlet. Something caught between the teeth. A bit of hair over the eye. The coldness of the glass. The wetness of it. Money. Our hands discovered all they could and would not be still. While we laughed at "The People" around us and knew we were not superior, but laughed anyway because we were nervous over what we knew about them and about ourselves through them.

Our hands that were here after being everywhere else. After being alive for thirty-four years, and educated. The hands that knew, by feel, more than we knew by thought. The automatic hands that had been dirty before and now were clean and out for an evening at the Somerset.

The Letter

He said he would be gone for about ten days and that he'd write. They looked at each other's faces during the whole waiting time, not taking their eyes off once lest they miss a moment which they would not be able to catch again. They looked and looked to accumulate it in order to distribute it over the time they wouldn't be able to look. And they touched. They held hands, held waists, they rested their arms on each others shoulders, they touched lips, and they leaned their sides together, gathering contact to make up for the time to come when they couldn't touch.

When the time was up he got on, throwing "write me" back over his shoulder, and when he appeared in the window of the scenic seat he threw her a kiss and she noticed how far his hair stood out from his head and she wanted to touch it and pat it down. She had not noticed it when he was close. When the train began to move she stood there getting smaller and smaller, seeing herself from his window, as he disappeared on the long silver form.

On the drive home she saw his eyes and mouth and cheekbones and remembered what he said. And she imagined the letter he would write and how he would mention love in it somewhere. She saw his smooth strong neck and smelled his soft thick hair, and changed lanes forgetting to turn on her signal.

She gave him two days and on the third she ran to the mailbox across the street and pulled open the metal door. Her chest was tight. She took the stack of envelopes like a card shark his deck and parted them in a fan and saw that his letter was missing. She walked back to her house without the speed she came with and thought that the letter was at the post office but they had overlooked it. There was a looseness where the tightness in her chest had been as she let up a little on her sureness. But she smiled because she knew why he hadn't written.

She saw him sitting on the train for those two solid days and being too nervous to write. The surroundings were too different. He was that way. He was easily upset, sensitive to his environment, needing things to be just right. She knew he had read instead, to relax. To escape. They had talked about that. She knew he had taken the small brown paper sack and went into the bathroom with it and tipped it up and swallowed a long shot of the whiskey they had bought together just for the trip so that he could sleep in the seat. She didn't know if he had rented a pillow or not. He might have used his jacket.

The next day she was sure about the letter. He would be home now with his mother who wanted him to be what he couldn't. And his sister would be laughing when he talked so he would say things to make her laugh some more. His younger brother would want to know about California and his older brother would want to know what he was going to do with his life. And he may have gone to visit his youngest brother's grave. The brother he used to wrestle and tease. And at night he would go to the room he used to have as a boy and he would have a need to write in order to talk to her because he would be missing her and needing to share all of his thoughts with her. He would have sat down by now to his old desk to tell her something on paper.

She watched the clock and gave it a good extra minute past eleven and then went out to the mailbox, looking at its grained wooden stand with the grass growing around the foot of it and marveled at the whole idea of mailboxes. She opened the door and saw at once that there was no letter.

She held the pamphlets and rural box holder ads with fingers that did not like the feel of the thickness and stiffness of big company paper. In the house she threw them on the desk and flopped down on the couch and sighed. The objects in the room moved in and crowded her. The walls and furniture were pressing in too close. She wanted to kick them and bust them. She jumped up and, with vulnerable knee caps which felt they would be bumped by a chair, she found herself flinging the chair out of her way and slamming out the front door. She walked until the anticipation that had built up for the letter was spent. And all the while she walked, a consolation was moving in and filling her head. She knew that tomorrow there would be a letter. For sure. The consolation came packaged without doubt. So she went home and sat down and wrote him a letter and mailed it that night, driving into town to the main post office, fifteen miles.

She saw him standing at his father's bedside and looking down at his father dying of cancer. She saw him crying later in his room on the same bed he had as a boy, where he had masturbated hundreds of times, and where his father had brought him buttered toast at six o'clock in the morning just to be with him before he went off to work. And in two days she knew that somewhere in his stuff he would have put her letter after reading it and having trouble reading it because of the messy ballpoint and her ragged sentences and he will be glad that she too had his letter.

His mother will be busy making him a chocolate pie and a roast beef dinner and he will be watching her, looking down because she is short , and his soft eyelashes will lay on his cheekbones the way they did when he looked down at her at the train station.

Tomorrow. It was a sure thing. She knew he would have had time by then and have missed her enough. He had visited with his family. He had visited the hospital. He had gotten settled in the new surroundings.

At eleven o'clock she opened the box. There was no letter. It was a foggy day. Back in the kitchen she threw a cup on the floor and watched it spray into a hundred pieces because the cup had defied her. It had hung onto her finger when she wanted to place it on the table. As she picked up the pieces she thought about him walking around over there fifteen hundred miles away and not writing to her. She decided to catch a plane, to surprise him with a phone call from a hotel near his house. But she crushed the idea as it formed because how could she compete with a dying father.

She was suddenly very tired. More tired than the mornings after they stayed up all night making love. The weariness gave weight to her arms and legs and because she did not want to move about they became bored. In the lethargy there was a restlessness that ticked away at her like a drip of water on the head. She lay on the couch and saw what she did not want to see, chairs, vases, ash trays, T.V., books. Pictures on the walls facing outward to be seen? By whom? Who wants to see them.

She lay on the couch a lot and slept during the day a lot. She walked a lot and looked at the mountains and the ocean. She liked to see things off in the distance instead of up close. And when the feeling of distance gave her an impression of beauty she said, "God damn it. Why can't he write."

After that she began to play voodoo with the mailbox. She thought if she let the mail sit there in the box a few hours, say until one, and she ignored it, there'd be a letter from him. She decided it was the way she had run out those first few days that had scared the letter away. To want something that much always brought bad luck. So with all her concentration she ignored the eleven o'clock mail delivery.

And for three more consecutive days there was no letter from him. She wondered if she'd be able to do her hair and put on a smile and look half radiant when he called for her to pick him up, if it ever came to that. A pimple came and went and she didn't think she would ever be able to hide the tiredness of her face even with the tint and glow blusher from Avon.

On the tenth day she got out her poison pen. She wrote him a note without an opening or a closing. It simply stated that she could not take his not writing and that was that. She drove like a robot to the big red, white and blue mail box on the corner and dropped it in. She felt better. It was better signing off, finishing up. Her mind was closed.

At eleven o'clock on the eleventh day she tried not to notice the time. She nonchalantly shuffled across the street and took the mail. She casually glanced through it and her eye caught the way one eight cent stamp looked, as if it were on a personal letter. She snatched it and looked and saw that it was an ad. Immediately she averted her eyes, pretending she hadn't looked. She tossed her head to off-set the shot of eagerness.

A hard lump settled in her chest. She said, "You bastard. You damn bastard," out loud and under her breath she said, "I miss you." She thought of the poison pen note on its way and even though she felt better having written it she decided to ward it off. She dialed him long distance with her heart beating so fast it made her breath come short in her throat. She did not know his family and how to explain who she was if they answered. He answered.

"Welllll, what a pleasure it is to hear your voice." It was the same voice she remembered he had.

"I miss you. Why haven't you written?" Her voice had become small and high.

"What a pleasure," he repeated.

"What are you thinking about?" she asked him with a begging undertone. "Is everything still the same?" She wanted to know about their love.

"No, he's worse off than they thought he was."

"I'm sorry," and she gave it time and then said, "Do we still love each other?"

"I still love you."

"And I love you, but I'm missing you so much. It's awful. How much do you love me?"

"Completely."

"Do you?"

"Yes."

"Why don't you write?"

"I should. I got your letter. It was terrific." She did not know what to say to him.

He said, 'This must be costing you a fortune."

"That's ok. I really miss you. Please write." Her voice had filled out a little but was still thinner than usual.

"I will tomorrow. Or tonight." She saw his adam's apple; it always moved when his voice sounded like that.

"Good. So will I. I love you. Goodbye."

"Goodbye love." And he hung up and left her with the buzz. She remembered she had forgotten to tell him about the bad note on its way.

She gave it two days. That's how long it would take if he wrote that night. But his letter did not come in two days. She took a deep breath and thought he must have sat up talking with his mother that night. But he promised to write the next day. Twenty-four hours more this time.

There was no letter the next day. She did not share her legs that night. The bristles rubbed together on her shins as she slept and she knew why a monk wore a hair coat. She did not remove the hair from her upper lip and she did not wash her feet after jogging in the dirt. She did not shower. And she did not dress well, or hope for the next eleven o'clock. She began mumbling, "Well, that's that. It's finished." And she began shrugging her shoulders.

As the second week drew to a close, she could no longer see his face. She could only see the idea she had of him, a big, warm friendly form, like in a dream. She became confused, or let herself indulge in confusion, that perhaps she had only dreamed him all along. She had never put him on a train and he had never gone away because he had never been.

The longing for him was longing for longing's sake. She liked to long because it gave her foresight. A chance to look forward to something. It had never been attached to him. He had merely been the excuse to get it going.

And on the sixteenth day she decided she did not want him to come back. If he did she would have to give up the longing and there he would be instead. He would not be as she remembered him. Not as handsome, not as big, not as perfect. Not as nice. She would be disappointed. She held onto her longing and looked at a photograph of him until it blurred. His skin would be merely skin and his hair merely hair. His eyes simply the eyes she would recall when seeing them again, as the eyes she saw at departure, not as the eyes she saw in her imagination during his absence. His neck would have limitations. In her mind it had no boundaries. Its smoothness and its strengths were epitomes of smooth, strong necks. It would be just another neck again when he appeared.

She thought of the love she would feel when she saw him, the strenuous aching love, and she wanted only to rest in the easy longing she felt now. The gentle, ever lessening longing which would soon vanish altogether and leave her empty and free from him. And then she would rest for a long time and wake up refreshed and alone, if he never came back and if he never wrote.

On the seventeenth day as soon as she awoke, she said out loud, "I know he is never going to write. I'm sure of it. Never." She packed her mind with negatives, not daring to admit that she knew intuitively that a certain number of negatives always caused a positive.

The letter came that day. When she saw it she had not even been thinking about it. She had been thinking about the loose tarred gravel in the street and how it hurt her feet. Her eyes landed on the small thin envelope and his handwriting and there was a sudden drop in her stomach like hitting a dip on a desert road. She had it open and was reading it before she got to the other side of the street, noticing the dash instead of a comma after her name, eagerly searching out his idiosyncrasies.

As she held it after reading it a touch of shame colored her. It was coming all the time. She glimpsed her opposite, a reserved, patient woman waiting stoically for a letter, trusting that it would come. She let it bite in awhile to free herself. And then she opened the letter again and read about their love.

He drops by. A simple gesture. And stabs me a thousand times with his mannerisms. The dog offers me his wounded leg and I am confused. He, and the dog, Alex, and everyone become the same. I want to lick a wound somewhere for someone. I touch the hairy foreleg of the German shepherd and it is His arm or Alex's leg. I am united through limbness. *General life-type limbs.*

The Sand Was All Over Them

The sand was all over them, on her cheeks, in his hair. They rolled around some more collecting the grains on their bodies and in the sweat of their palms as they touched each other. A wind came up and blew sand in their eyes and mouths. They ground it between their teeth and she leaned into his ear with her shoulder bumping his and said, 'Since it's such a wretched day, let's remember all the best times. The very best. I'll start."

He looked into the sand and did not acknowledge that he was in agreement or not. "I liked the time you were standing outside in the parking lot waiting for me by my car, and your eyes were brown and there was a look in them that I liked. It wasn't sad or happy. It was one of wanting something, but with a take it or leave it glint. I liked that, and that you had found my car and waited for me."

There was only the feeling of the wind and the sand hitting their faces and the sound of the ocean hitting the beach. "Your turn," she said, wanting to go home and never see him again.

He began slowly. He always spoke slowly and enunciated each word by itself. There was never a slurring of words together when he spoke because he had to speak carefully in order to avoid getting stuck on a word. His mother had taken him to a hypnotist as a child to try to cure him of stuttering. She had tried everything except getting off of his back, because his soul had to end up in the Catholic heaven even if it meant the sacrificing of his tongue. "I liked the time, after that first night when we planned to meet for coffee the next morning, and you weren't there, and I thought shit, and then you came out of a store and you were wearing a dress and I saw your legs. It was

24

the first time and they were beautiful and you were smiling. And your teeth are fantastic."

"I remember," she said.

"And I thought you wouldn't be there. That you'd have second thoughts or be too embarrassed to come."

She put her arm around his back and rubbed his sandy neck with her sandy hand. It was nice to bury her fingers in his warm sunny hair. He leaned on his elbows and continued to look into the sand.

"Our feelings were tender then, weren't they?" she said. "What happened?" They both laughed as if it were a joke.

"I remember our having coffee at that outside café all those times and how funny you were. And I couldn't stop laughing." She picked a bump off of his arm. He jerked his arm away from her.

"I'll get cancer." He looked at the place and rubbed it and saw that it was beginning to bleed. "What became of those coffees," he said, mumbling it between lips that pressed downward to allow him to look at the bump she had just picked off.

"We changed vicinities, that's all," she said wanting to run away from him, to get away from the death of it, the ending of what ever they had had. "And stop being so careful with yourself. You will never get cancer." She rubbed her hand over him again searching for another bump.

"Your turn," she said.

He didn't want to go on. She waited and he said, "We used to meet here every Sunday and go for a long walk down the beach. Why'd we stop?"

She rested her face on her sandy arm and turned it so he couldn't see it. She believed it was because she was not beautiful, or not the most beautiful of all. And because she did not have big breasts. She believed those things would have held him. Or money. One or the other, beauty or money. Or talent. Or a great wit. She knew he could not be expected to love her for nothing. She could not love herself for nothing.

It had made her uncomfortable all those months when he had told her he loved her. It seemed right suddenly for him to stop saying it. He should only love an epitome of something and never just an ordinary person. She had told him that and he tried to argue with her. But he had to agree after awhile when she insisted that people settle for one another because they have no choice. But that they should not pretend to love each other.

She tried to sleep because she did not want to talk to him anymore. She had said everything she would ever say to him and all the rest would be to keep a noise going for the effect of friendship, but it would all be repetition. And he had told her all he would ever tell. Perhaps it was that instead of the beauty. They had simply run out of new things to say to each other.

What could she say to him after a year of saying everything she wanted him to know. She had told him that she never got her fill of blackberries. He had told her that he loved pound cake. She had told him never to smash a bug because it was too easy and it took something special not to. He had told her that he used to be affected by everything, even riding a bus and seeing a strange face, a deformed face out the window would make him nauseous. That everything was a gut feeling with him. She had said it was that way with her too.

But what did she say to her husband? It had been nine years and they had not yet run out of things to say. They spoke about the things they had to do together for their children and the home and their future. There was never an end to what they would say. It would go on even past their deaths and people would say it for them after that. Their children and their children's children and maybe other people too.

But with him there was nothing more to say. She had told him what she liked and disliked and the way she had grown up and what mattered to her and what didn't. He had told her all the same things about himself. They had communicated with their compassion through it all. They had understood. The "savvy" had flowed between them like the right amount of oil in the gears and they had "grooved." For about twelve months the savvy ran thick and smooth. The hippie vocabulary was seeping into the mainstream.

The dryness of the beach stiffened the creases at the corners of their eyes. Her hand lay in the sand beneath his nose, under his steady gaze It was brown and full of veins. She said, "Does the visage of that delicate lovely white thing excite you. Does it speak of femininity? Does it smack of promises of softer things somewhere else?" Her throat was tight holding back laughter.

He suddenly looked up and said, "I didn't know you were a brick layer." She lay laughing and weak beside him in the sand, biding time until two-thirty when she would have to go home and be there in time for the school bus.

The death of their joy in being together hung between them. She said, "Let's walk."

"No," he yelled, faking anger. She pretended to pound on his back with her fists. "I don't want to walk," he said with his bottom teeth coming up.

"I don't want to just thrash around in this sand," she yelled back.

"It's grimy isn't it?" He got up and began brushing off his shoulders and arms. She helped by scrubbing into the hairs on his stomach to get the sand out beneath them.

"Ow," he stepped back and she dropped her hand and stood there surprised.

"But there's sand there."

"I'll have to take a shower," he said. He whipped his fingers gingerly through the thick windy hair on his head. "Jesus," and he held his hands away from himself as if the sand was seagull shit on his fingers.

As they walked up the hill toward the car she said, "It was good that we didn't walk this time, huh? Because when we do there's always a point we're heading for and after we get that far then we turn around and come back and it's all over. It's timed when we walk. It was good to just flop down and have no plan wasn't it? Just anywhere. Isn't there something to that?"

"I think you've hit on it baby," he said, looking in her direction but not into her eyes and freezing his face into acceptability.

She laughed because she still liked telling him exactly what she felt. It had become ridiculous. Even now at the end she could not let it go. Even now when he had grown tired of her perceptions she could not stop baring her seeping insights to him. Perhaps it wasn't that they had run out of things to say after all. Maybe it WAS the beauty thing.

They got into the hot car and opened the windows. "What became of the big Feeling, capital big, capital F e e l i n g." She spelled it. It was their current joke, to capitalize important words and make them stand for titles, and categories.

"Capital S H I T," he spelled. They drove away laughing with abandon. He opened the car roof with an impatient fist. "Let's let the world in," he yelled and the wind sailed through and grabbed her hair. The air was hot and she felt well cared for in its warmth and safe, even though she could not settle on the reason they were no longer enthusiastic about each other.

She said, "I wish we were on our way to Mexico," and at the same time she wanted her kitchen sink for an anchor.

"And we had everything we needed packed away back there," he said glancing at the back seat with eyes that imagined seeing the baggage.

"Yes, and I was about eighteen." She glanced at him. "And blonde." He smiled at her.

"If you were eighteen and blonde you wouldn't be here with me."

"What are you saying?" she squealed, "that I'm here with you because I'm not young and good looking. That we're settling for what we can get. That we have no choice?" She was not glad that she had caught him. Maybe it was beauty after all.

"No," he said, continuing on with the trip to Mexico. "We

could stop anywhere and do what we wanted. When we were tired of a place we would just move on."

"Yes," she said. "It would be fun but what about all the things I need, like to do my hair?" She wanted to be in her bathroom where all the things she needed to make herself presentable were. She edged away from the trip to Mexico as he drove carefully down the frontage road to her house. He looked over at her and did not understand what she had asked.

"I need a lot of things now that I'm older," she said. "I can't just take off and be free anymore. I need a lot of stuff. I don't hold together without my environment anymore." He looked back at the road. "There was a time when I could have bummed around. When I didn't need anything."

He pulled up to her yard. He kissed her and did not let her go for awhile. She still liked his breath. He sighed, and took his big hand from the back of her head. "I'll give you a call tomorrow," he said and drove away. She was glad to get back to her sink, where he could rest easy in her mind.

When she was with him the sink pushed into her mind. Perhaps it was not lack of beauty or lack of things to say. Maybe it was the sink.

3.

I Went to the Zoo to Let the Elephants See Me
After the affair was over, he lay in his grave, and
she longs to be seen by him again.

I Went to the Zoo to Let the Elephants See Me

I wanted to go somewhere. I wanted to *be* somewhere. I wanted to *be there* and to *be someone*. I wanted to *be someone being there*. And to *be seen being someone there*. So I went to the zoo.

Before I went I saw myself being there and people seeing me there. And people seeing me knowing something about the animals there. And I felt the aloneness I would feel alone among the people. Set apart from them. And it is what I wanted. It seemed right. And out of all the people there would be someone who had been looking for me. Who had come there to find me. I saw myself being discovered at the zoo.

I saw myself bending down to sniff a flower in the sunshine, and my brown hair having golden highlights, and when I turned (in mid-sniff) there would be a man watching me. He would have blue eyes and grooves in his cheeks and other than that he is faceless, but he sees me and sees into me, and does not take his eyes off me. There is the command of *discovery* in him. He has discovered the qualities he has been looking for all his life (because, of course, I am a nymph and the flower is in the woods and there is no background to define me socially). He sees a basic human female. A true and perfect being. And there I am being found by *the male*. A male who *knows*.

So I went to the zoo, drove there in my truck and parked and walked up the long entrance way, taking my time, striding in wood soles and pantlegs and it felt right. My loneness. The ability to be found. The qualification, of being lost, so that it was right to be found. And I thought of the time when I had been found before. When I was *someone somewhere*, and the sadness over being lost again filled me just right. I wore the sadness and the loneness as a cloak, daring anyone to strip it off me or to peek under it and see me hiding inside, believing they could not find me that easy because I would hide as hard as they would look, because of the memory of being found once and then lost again. The new finding would have to be intense and thorough in order to prove its lasting strength.

The aura encompassed me like a fur. I snuggled inside and saw men glancing. Their eyes told of their loneliness too, alongside their wives or friends, or holding the hand of their child. Seeing their loneliness while they walked with people made me look away. I envisioned them walking with me and looking lonely to someone else and the possibility of having their loneliness alongside me made me know I would be almost impossible to find again.

As I walked, I tried to be oblivious to being seen. I did not want to appear to notice people seeing me. I wanted to show the world that I was bombarded with glances but that it all passed by me. And I wanted to see all the people knowing that about me.

I went to the elephants first. I wanted to see their grayness. So I stood there a long time with my arms folded looking at them, watching their trunks swing and blow and move constantly, and I tried to feel the impact I thought I would get from seeing a trunk that I did not have. To see it dangle off a face the way it didn't dangle off mine. I wanted to know of tremendous weight and to look at the four stump feet that were able to hold it. I wanted to fear being crushed. I wanted to see their weapon. The weight. I wanted to see them knowing about their own weapon, playing with it, having it, being caught up in it. I looked at their size and color and movement and I tried to feel something about their being trapped by what they were and unable to do anything about it. But I couldn't. I could not even know about their separateness. There was no impact.

I looked at the people and knew that none of us can know about an elephant. We could never know their difference. It would never come to us. We didn't have it in us to know about *difference* and *sameness*. So I moved on to look at the goats, hugging myself with Indian arms.

I saw the capybaras on the way, and made myself remember *the man who had discovered me once*. We had seen them together two years before and he had told me of floating up a river in Bolivia and being so bored that he had sat there on the boat and shot bullets into capybara along the way. And I had shrieked at him, "You mean you just splatted bullets into the sides of the poor animals and left them to suffer. You didn't even eat them?"

"We ate one," he told me. "One some other guy shot. But, yes, I was bored. I know. It sounds bad." And he let it go at that. But after that I thought of him as a Chicago city guy who did not feel a kinship with animals and I never trusted him as much because of it. To hurt something in that way. Aimless. Out of boredom. For his pleasure. Passing by. Target practice. And I wanted him to repent somehow by telling me he knew better now and would never do it again. But he didn't.

It was too obvious, thinking about him when I saw the capybara. It was cheap. It was on cue. It was lazy. It happened every time by association and I could have made myself not think of him. It was an indulgence. I did not respect myself when I did so because he should get more than that from me. I should feel more than what memory evoked. More than a sense of loss. A loss of his audience, of not being seen by him anymore, of not being able to perform for him again.

I watched a father showing his toddler daughter a small goat. They were inside the farmyard. His bravery reigning over her timorousness petted me. And I stayed there and stared, watching their gentle movements which were all occurring in one small space. There was no running or wild gesturing. The father simply squatted and took her tiny fat hand and held it under the goat's nose to be nuzzled, and when she pulled away and squeezed tighter between his knees for safety, his arms shielded her and his laughter was silent and he remained unafraid, a safe fort. I pulled my eyes away after awhile and walked on to the mink. They climbed into a barrel and left me looking at a bare tree stump in their cage.

I saw a man walking around with a camera and I believed he had taken a picture of me when I wasn't looking and that he caught me in action, caught my essence. But as he passed by he didn't even look, so I let it go, the idea that my image was an interesting subject to him. And I did not like him much.

I walked past the puma and the apes and the snakes and turtles and glanced at the alligators and at a young man with a girlfriend. The beautiful faces of youth caused me to want to pull a curtain down over my own face which suddenly grew conspicuous. I wanted to cover it up out of embarrassment that I was just a lady to them. I wanted more from them. It would matter if young people felt more than that. It would matter more than being liked by old people. I wanted to still matter to the young. Not mattering was *being nowhere* and *no one*.

Having passed by youth gave strength to my aloneness. I thought of walking beside *the man who had discovered me* and seeing his eyes shift to a newer face, and I was glad he had prevented that, at least.

I watched the seals, and I saw a man watching me out of the corner of my eye. I was excited by it. A flash passed through me and I believed it was the person who understood me, standing there smoking, drinking a machine cup of coffee, biding his time, knowing all that *must* be known about me in order to love me. Like God. A man seeing the quality that lets him know what I try to hide, my *goodness*. I turned, self-conscious, and looked to see who was actually watching me. He was a heavy-set man with purple levis and carrot red hair. And he was more undesirable than if I hadn't anticipated someone else. He could not know about me even if I *told* him. He knew *nothing* or only of going to be zoo because he had nothing else to do with his life. And of watching me. He was a thug and all the other things his big pink body told me about.

I walked away, distressed that I didn't know better. Who comes to the zoo, anyway? So I went down to see the lion. He slept with his hind quarters toward me and I looked at his soft furry testicles for a long time and felt sorry for him. I whistled once, and read the sign which said *Do Not Tease the Lion*. And in my silent watching I began to believe that I was being watched. I glanced around but there was no one.

I stood in front of the macaws cage and watched it eat a section of orange, and its slow methodical movements massaged me and I leaned against the rail, bracing my thighs and watched until I lost interest. A blackbird walked on top of the cage and the macaw turned its head and cast a black eye upward at the bird, and I wanted to tell *the only man* to see the way the macaw had to turn its head to look up. And for him to copy it so I could laugh and laugh and double over laughing, holding onto his big leg-of-lamb arm, and loving him for making me laugh. But I put it out of mind.

I went past all the rest of the cages and looked at the capybaras again on my way toward the entrance. And then I left.

4.

Sometimes At Night, Yearning in the Midst,
and **Soft and Sad Over The Whiteness**
are about her trying to get perspective about time
passing and everything changing.

Sometimes At Night:

She has gone outside before, at night. Slipped out through
a crack in the door into the quiet night. Away from the
heat and noise and confusion and disappeared in the
dark walking under the black sky. And then she has come
back and approached her house on Indian feet. Stalked
it. Stealthily. On the balls of her feet. To see what kind of
thing it was. She has peered in through its yellow windows,
one window at a time, and saw the contents of it with
night eyes, roaming cat eyes. Wild, lost, not owned animal
eyes. And she saw that it was any house anywhere. She has
seen a man sitting in there. He is any man anywhere. In a
chair on any given night at any given time. She has seen
this man laugh alone in front of a television screen. And
she has felt a million miles away. Many centuries away, as
she stood there looking in her window at her husband in
his chair. Inside the strange, wilderness place, taking a nice
ride through time and space.

She has paced around the yard, playing with the house.
Glancing at it from different angles, letting it tell her things.
And it has spoken to her in the dark, with daylight padding
blotted out. It has spoken of its stuffing. The things inside
it. Private things. Markings. Things that give evidence. Of
her. Of all people. That she lives at all. That they all do.
She, female, and the implements of her existence. And
then she has gone back inside because she was cold.

A Yearning in the Midst

Ina died. At forty-two. Before she was ready. Before any of us were ready. And after wearing all that make-up, and high fashioned hair-dos. She left jars and bottles and flasks and vials and boxes and plastic snap-on containers of mascara, foundation, moisturizers, cleansers, lip dew, masks, eye liner, rouge, powder, and blushers on her dresser at home as she lay head shaved, and bare-faced on an operating table an incision in her skull.

We were all waiting to see what Ina would do with old age. Ina, who had the tiniest voice of us all. And the biggest breasts. Who would have married her rabbi in the twinkling of an eye. Whose youngest daughter goes around with a shaved head to break through the pretensions of her mother's hair styles, and now cannot bear to look upon her mother's dead bare shaved and naked head.

Everyone showed up for the funeral. Miriam, Alice, Dean, Dale, Davy, Ruth and even Naomi. All the sisters and brothers and their spouses and their children. Ina's two daughters, Pam and Marjourie Ann were there. And the mother of them all, Helen. At seventy-five, Helen was still wearing the fashionable clothes of a thirty-five year old woman. She had a high coif of black shiny curls upon her head. "Helen" is always written on the appointment book of some beauty shop with X's marked in to leave an hour's worth of time for beauty treatment. Shampoo and set, conditioner, trim, manicure, pedicure, facial, or removal of unwanted hairs. Helen has never put away the photographs of Ina in a ballet tutu at four. And Ina in a cowgirl suit on a pony at six, and Ina with a shock of curls in a pinafore at the piano looking like Shirley Temple at twelve. All the photos of Ina and identical ones of her other children sit on the knick knack shelves of a small retirement apartment, the way they sat on the mantle above the fireplace in her home thirty-five years before, when she was a young mother bustling with the promise of her children's futures. All the lessons. All the excitement. All the plans. They were going to be ballerinas, pianists, movie stars, mommies, models. One became a beautician. All of them got divorced. Half of them got vasectomies and hysterectomies. Ina worked in a pizza parlor and knew all the names of all the movie stars and what kind of emollients they used on their skins, and if they had any Jewish blood or not. She liked to feel a kinship. She bought the same brand of make-up. She called them "stars" and talked about "their skin," as if it were her own. Her big near-sighted brown eyes would twinkle with the joy of her research through movie magazines.

Someone said they thought Ina ate too much pizza and not enough salad was what killed her. She was buried next to her father, Sam, who had died after six heart attacks, one each year toward the last, losing his temper in court. He was an attorney who could not work hard enough to provide make-up, clothes and beauty parlor appointments for his beautiful wife and beautiful daughters.

Ina, my half-aunt who used to brush my hair when I was ten and she was twenty. Who pulled and yanked and had no patience with my knots until my eyes watered. Ina, who looked at me in terms of what I could do to fix myself up. Pull back my hair. Lower my blouse. Shave my legs. Pluck my brows. Bleach my freckles. Rub Helena Rubenstein's moisturizer into my elbows. Wash my feet and wear sandals. Gold ones. With little straps.

Ina, who never drank or smoked or learned to drive. Who rode the Greyhound bus from Bakersfield to Hollywood once a month to go to the Oceanic Room, wearing white Palm Springs slacks and a low cut blouse, hoping to catch a glimpse of a "star" and ask her what kind of cosmetics she used. And match cleavages.

Ina, who married a forty-year-old jockey named Buzz at

sixteen because he wasn't from Bakersfield and had a gold ring on his little finger and knew the names of rich men and their horses and had seen Virginia Mayo in person at the race track. She divorced him at twenty-five because he wanted her to get up and fix his breakfast and clean the house and change the babies. She wanted to go to the mirror and put on her face.

I still have a silk summer blouse Ina forgot at my house. I am in awe of it. A Hollywood blouse I would never wear. Could not wear even if I would. A sexy cleavage kind of blouse. It's a kind of souvenir of somewhere I've never been.

For as long as I can remember there was Ina. Posing in photographs. With my father and mother. And then alone with my father. In those little photographs you take at bus depots. Grinning. Sparkling. Smiling and giggling by his side. The young half-sister who came to visit every summer. The beautiful Ina whose shiny black hair and snow white skin never showed traces of being touched by the sun. The beautiful Ina who had bad breath. It was the incongruity of it. Like a rose with thorns. She had to brush her tongue with toothpaste and gargle with mouth wash but was never able to get rid of bad breath.

Buzz married her anyway and began drinking. They had two daughters. The youngest shaved her head and went to live with another woman. The oldest married a man with no legs, home from the war. She wanted to care about something besides tweezing her brows. She turned to Jehovah and became a witness and pushed her half-man around in a wheelchair and eventually had a baby. Ina was a grandmother. Working in a pizza house, riding the Greyhound, dating a bartender who fed goldfish to his piranhas. She pasted on longer and longer eyelashes.

And sometimes she babysat for her grandson. That's where they found her. On the floor of her daughter's beautiful home with her beautiful face pressed against the rug. Her shiny black coif unruffled. White slacks intact. Fingernails and toenails silvered. Cleavage under purple silk. Perfumed. The doctors said it was a brain hemorrhage. Helen said it was a good thing she wasn't holding the baby.

All that glitter. Underground. We laughed briefly, my sister and I who go easy on the Hollywood image. "It was probably a cold cream clot on the brain." And then we go solemn, ashamed, wondering what we will do now, without Ina around to dream of Hollywood and the stars and tend her milk-white cleavage, and false eyelashes. Who will believe in all those things for us now. Who will have that simple innocent yearning in the midst of our cynicism and naturalism?

Soft And Sad Over the Whiteness

My mother and father sit in the same room. I serve them cherry wine in stemmed glasses. My mother holds her delicate glass with a workworn hand. A plump and strong sun-browned hand, and her little finger helps balance the glass. It has no pretensions; but the upward tip of her chin as she smiles and speaks to my father tells of her wanting to communicate the message of, "Look at us now. Would you have believed it twenty years ago."

My father has traveled three hundred and fifty miles just to sit in my living room and sip wine and look uncomfortable and overly tactful. He is an old world man. It is another man's house. He has driven carefully, ever watchful of the horror of a car accident. He will tell about a car accident he saw once before he leaves. His white hair causes my mother's face to go soft and sad. She has not seen him for several years, not since the last time they met accidentally in my house.

They have been divorced sixteen years. They were married twenty-five. They sit and sip up in their future. They have already said all the things to each other that couples say. About love, about fear, about sorrow, about anger, and then about hate. They have already experienced as many variations of the sexual act that their small town morals allowed them. Years ago. And held each other tenderly or passionately or indifferently. Years ago.

They have already thrown a dish or two, slammed doors to shut the other out, yelled or stomped around in despair. Years ago. My mother has already plummeted her strong brown fists on my father's thin nicotine chest. He has already tried to slap her and has already torn his hand open on the wedding ring he gave her fifteen years before, and had to lie down when he saw the blood. She has already thrown a pound of lard on the floor so that the sides of the box split and white clean lard shot out and stuck to the linoleum. She has already shouted that she didn't want lard. She wanted Crisco.

He has already reared up out of his chair like a troll from the kitchen table and raised his plateful of food above his head and slammed it face down on the linoleum beside the lard and shouted back to shut up and quit nagging.

Yet they sit and sip cherry wine and chit chat. In my house. She has gotten too fat. He has gotten too thin. And her eyes go soft and sad over the whiteness of his hair and the badness of his teeth. Her voice is like chirping birds. She has already sung opera with the radio while hanging out his blue work shirts and all those diapers. In the sunshine. Years ago.

He has already driven her to ballets and concerts and movies and let her off at the curb and picked up her later, sitting and smoking and waiting the car at midnight. She has already danced out of the theaters with her eyes wet from tears and gotten in beside him and rolled down the window to let the smoke out. Years ago. He has already taken her home and ignored the beauty and romance that filled her heart after music and dance, and taken her body in an unromantic and unbeautiful way. Years ago.

They sit and sip now and I move about bringing them things. Treats. It is a pleasure for me to give them whatever I have, knowing they have never had enough. Even I do not, cannot, give them what they need. Cannot make up for all the not having they have had.

My father grows relaxed after the first few sips of wine. His eyes are gentle and kind but wise. They are on the look-out. He remembers how my mother can be. And she remembers too. They do not leave themselves open. There are too many things they have left unresolved and will never be able to resolve. They will have no defense against these things and will go on trying to win against the other if they are brought up. About whether he ever helped fold diapers or not. Or if oranges are all that good for you or not. And how he would never stop at a fruit stand by the side of the road when they were on a trip in the car.

I still remember their shouts and red faces. Their threats to leave each other and find a perfect mate. Years ago. I move between them now the way I always moved between them, without stirring what is between them.

They sit and sip. They have time to relax. It has already happened between them. All the need. All the demands. All the indulgences. All the present getting. Years ago.

They have already harmonized their voices in song. Singing *Home on the Range, Down in the Valley, Casey Jones, You Are My Sunshine*, or *I'll Take You Home Again Kathleen*. Years ago. She has already stood ironing dozens of his shirts until her legs broke out in varicose veins. She crosses her ankles now and the nylons she wears suppress and conceal some of the blue of the veins. He has already gotten up at six a.m. for forty years and gone off to work and brought home paycheck after paycheck. They have already fought and clawed and scratched over the paltry coins and dollar bills like two jungle creatures over a find of bananas. Years ago.

They sit and sip and my mother's eyes go soft and sad over my father's white hair. After awhile her hand reaches out to him and her fingers touch his hair. She sighs. So much has passed. Even pigment. He lets her pet him. He is the small male. She is the large female. Like the frail nervous sperm and the large ample safe ovum.

I spoil the moment by reaching for my camera. My mother withdraws her hand. She is married. She has been married a second time for as long as I have the first.

They sit and sip. In the same room. They have already been together in rooms for twenty-five years, sixteen years ago. My mother's eyes go soft and sad over the whiteness of his hair and the darkness of his teeth. She has already said there was no hair darker and no teeth whiter than his. Years ago. And he has already said there was no woman as beautiful as she was. Years ago.

It's the way my mother's eyes go soft and sad over the whiteness of his hair that scares me.

> *Alex put everything on wheels. All of his machines in the shop and some of the furniture in the house and some things in the yard. He dreams of planes and boats and submarines and space ships. Vehicles of escape, of getting away. Of going somewhere. And all the while he keeps being there beside me. Past my believing it. Past my expectations. Convincing me. Becoming spiritual. His familiarity. While he puts everything on wheels. Beside me. All around me. Wheels.*

5.

Noel In My House, The Kiss, The Graph In The Sky,

are about her knowing what men need to stay excited over life, and she knows she could save them from their lackluster desperation, but doesn't. She sees the trade-off of youth for knowledge, and wonders if its worth it.

Noel

Noel sits in her house. Beside her. With his white soft arms and legs folded gently. And his soft lazy belly, his forty-five year old man's belly pushing out not with fat but with tired forty-five year old posture. They sit side by side watching television while Katie, the wife, is on an errand, driving in her car. He watches an old movie while she watches him from the corner of her eye, wondering what it is that keeps them from each other. Why they did not touch as soon as Katie left. Because he is a man and she is a woman. A brother-in-law. A strange man. No blood. They would not have idiots for off-spring. They would not have anything. They would not do it for a baby. But because he is a man who is tired.

They would touch each other for therapy. Because he needs something besides his wife. Beside his work. Beside his home and children. Beside television. Beside his calmness.

She had watched him eat toast that morning. Without vitality. Without hunger. Without saliva or appetite. It simply went down into him because it was *breakfast*. Time to eat it. She watched, fascinated by his lethargy, swelling with energy by contrast. His eating toast was a matter of his sitting without sinew, softly on his chair. His small soft thighs pressing flat against the chair while he lifted his cup of coffee and piece of toast alternately. Sipping and grinding and swallowing and staring at nothing. Without a rigorous ripple of the jaw muscle.

It was the first time she had seen him after five years. And it was then that she wanted to go to him and help him. Even if it was to worry him, bother him, anger him. She wanted to see evidence of movement in him. So she tried to arouse it in him. She talked, trying to make him know things and to laugh at the way they were. She tried to save him in that one moment. And she believed she was obligated to because she alone detected the amount of dying he was doing. She believed she could save him. By making him laugh. At himself. At his lethargy. And to separate him from it. So she told him about her mother's cure for swallowing fish bones. And how she used to have to choke on psychosomatic ones to please her mother and allow her to give the white bread cure. She drew verbal pictures of great hunks of fluffy white bread with a fish bone sticking in it, even though it had already been chewed up and swallowed. And she watched Noel's face crease up, taking it's familiar contours of humor.

Noel had wanted to be an actor of comedy once. In his student days. He wrote plays. She went on to encourage his face and eyes to laugh some more because she felt power in it, making a sad man laugh. But remembering a man telling her once, "God, if I had only known she thought that much of herself, that she would be doing me a favor… " The memory of that man's anger over one woman's ego frightened her, but she could not help herself. In the same way as that woman, she thought Noel needed saving.

She had continued within loose ragged comments at the breakfast table until she destroyed his silence. At her end of the table she leaned on her elbows in his direction while he saw round-shouldered, soft-bellied, gray-haired, ashen-faced and loose-jawed, loving comedy. A remnant of him still loving comedy, wanting to laugh.

As he made comments back she saw the imperceptible bouncing of his head in mild-mannered laughter. A remnant of his former joy, reduced to good manners, after twenty years of government parties, cocktail chatter, teas and the CIA affairs on his mind.

He sits beside her now, alone with her. Left alone. And he moves in a sensual way. His toes, moving like a cat's paws when it's petted. He pets his mouth, a random two-fingered gesture. Over and over. Male and female have become aware of each other. But they wait.

She remembers how he sat all day smoking his pipe or small cigars. She saw the pipe cleaners and thought someone was doing to do a craft. He made a pastime of cleaning the pipe and refilling it, cupping one palm under the bowl of it to light it. And of puffing on it to get it started. And of settling back, half-lidded, pacified, biting it with his teeth ever so slightly while he puffed. His mother's nipple still somewhere in his heart. She saw the dark grains of carbon in her white sea shell ash trays. It startled her. She was not used to it. Her eyes were accustomed to cigarette butts with filters and a few thin flimsy gray ashes. And raw, whiskey -colored tobacco showing from an over-crushed cigarette. The harsh blackness of carbon matched Noel's shiny government casual shoes. A government worker on vacation. At her house. In California. Washington D.C. shoes on her floor. Slip on hard shoes with white ribbed pull-up socks. His idea of California. Of casualness. The kind she wore in high school. The kind she put a penny in. No straw or leather things for his pale indoor feet with their tender soles. Soles so thin she could have studied his circulatory system through them. And she believes they are cold feet. And that his hands are cold too. With blue veins barely visible. No bulging veins. Veins what never had to bulge. Typewriter hands. Briefcase hands. And that it would take a long time for him to be warm. To get a vigorous movement of his body going. A vigorous hip movement.

She studies his fingernails as he sips a gin and tonic that evening, and watches an old movie. A busy, proper, formal old movie. They are clean nails. They have not been dirty for a long time. Except from a bit of carbon paper or typewriter ribbon. Probably never from soil. But maybe from rebuilding antique furniture. They have been dirty with sawdust and glue from reviving a Pennsylvania dough board. She knows that as a fact. And he has probably hit one with a hammer. One of his delicate ridged fingernails that has not felt blood surging through it since the last time it was hit. His blood races only in pain. Never in exhilaration.

She sees his hands on her. Doing what men's hands do on women. Nipping, plunging, gliding along, sensing the structure as a whole. Her form. Or holding her hips, hanging on. And her stomach begins to churn. She is silently nauseated, seeing his tiredness on her. Feeling his fingers fumble, unsure. She loses some desire to save him. She imagines him SAVED and she sees no change in him. His posture the same. His soft white belly the same. His clean nails the same. His thin thighs the same.

She images that he leans over to touch her now with his white cool arms. His black casual shoes crossing each other sprawling on their sides against the vinyl floor to allow him to reach her. And later, after a soft, stale kiss. A lack luster exploration of her mouth, a tired pressurized examination of her mouth with his tongue she would try to detect evidence of life in his lap. She would find his tired member erect, but teetering, not sure, subject to die at the slightest hint of hesitation.

She falters, not sure if she can save him. The tediousness of keeping him going. She grows tired thinking of it. The hard work of it. She sees the black hairs jutting from his forearm. She knows he has hairs on his shoulders and back. She has seen him in a bathing suit. And saw his animal hairs against his putty human flesh. A monkey gone civilized. The hair laying wasted. Flattened under a cotton government shirt. Rubbed thin with the small sanding movements of reaching for his tobacco pouch, for a gin and tonic, a book, typing paper, a match, or a light off a friend. Hair breaking loose as he reaches for his attaché case, a document on the other side of a table across from his leather swivel chair. The hairs scraping this way and that with the movements of his body. Not jungle movements. Not free movements. Until finally each hair is weakened and breaks off.

His wife finding them everywhere. In the bed. Against the sheets. In the washing machine. On the bathroom tile. Her male mate shedding for twenty years alongside of her until she no longer notices the black animal hairs any more. She has stopped trying to wash each one down the drain.

She feels an imaginary one inside her mouth now as she sits beside him on the couch. One of his musk scented pubic hairs, and she takes her eyes away from his visage and watches the old movie. And waits.

His wife does not come. She wishes she would come back to take away what is there when she is gone. But there is no sound of her car and after awhile his fraility comes to her again. His absence of force. His missing aggression. And she is filled with a need to show him how to keep from dying. To arouse him. To bring color to his face. To warm his cat like feet. Or at least to let him know that she *would* want to warm them. That he *could* be desired. That he does not go unnoticed.

His presence wears on her until she hears a car drive up. And in comes his wife. The wife smiles and sits sweetly beside him. She has been known to have said, "Noel is a weak father figure." He does not look up when she enters. He shifts his weight to one side. And she notices he is an inch closer to her, away from where his wife has sat.

She can see herself like a slippery seal as they try to hold her away from what she wants. She can see them pressing their fingers into her slick and slippery hide as she slithers toward what she wants. And she can see them hooking her with a sharp instrument to keep her away from what she wants.

She is lying beside herself one morning. Seeing herself sprawled in bed. Not wanting to make an effort to move even one inch. Knowing only part of her is a body with limbs. Sensing her body as an animal would find it in the forest, sniffing and investigating it. A form on a mattress. With orifices. Smells and weight and textures. Position. But not her. Knowing about the form she casts but being separate. But being here. Anyway. And being caught there. Caught being what she is there. Aware of being there and nowhere else. Knowing it is impossible to be anywhere else if she is there. (Feeling) in one spot. Sticking out in time and place and space there. Knowing she does not know more than what being there and being what she is there can know. And wanting to escape the familiarity of it. Wanting to triumph over being there. Wanting to know more than being there. Wanting to have being there in her power. Not to be under the power of being there.

And sound things. A bird seeps in, hammering its song across the new grass and bright sun yards. Then sounds of people. Things moving. Doing. I am an insect hearing other insects cracking off straw stems, dragging stones, walking six-legged steps. On the deck I am a size definition. A bug size definition. A larger foot could crush me. A larger unit of thumb and finger could pinch me and roll me to death. I am an ant and my deck is all the rooms under the ground.

Someone has an idea for a costume. Say, at Carrows. But the costume is defeated because of individual differences. It becomes what it was not intended to be. The waitress's boots slip down and they all look like pirates.

The Kiss

I remember the wet desperate kiss of a drunk man once. A man who died a few years later, but on a holiday night staggered around the inside of his house without a mask, looking as if he wore one, the most gruesome one from Thrifty drug store. The one with the mouth turning down but not in mock tragedy.

When we knocked he answered too fast, turning the door knob with a great knob of a fist and carrying a glass of clear liquid and ice in the other hand. He was the father and husband of a friend and her daughter who had just left him.

Trick-or-treating him was both kind and unkind on my part. I knew he was lonely but I also knew it was no time for tricks. We entered his house, which, without his wife and daughter, had become a trap. He could not leave. There were payments. He had nowhere to go. Things were strewn about as if he had been fighting ghosts. Sounds bellowed from his barrel-shaped diaphragm in greetings he didn't feel. They came as groans of relief that someone had come upon his misery and might help.

He went into the kitchen to find something for the kids, and for me he brought out a glass dripping with gin and tonic. I refused and then accepted, feeling out my relationship to him now. There had been a time when I had thought of putting my arms around him and offering him something of myself, whatever I might represent to him, a viable lifestyle now that his had become out-dated. It was a time when I would stroll up the street with my tiny daughters to visit his tiny daughter. We would listen to their laughter and he would open up his door and allow me to see where he worked. A makeshift study in a rebuilt garage room. His typewriter on a small makeshift desk. Books along the walls on boards supported by bricks. Books about business. And his tales of having been in advertising, of having owned his own airplane, a hillside home, a sports car. All his knowledge and ownership coming to me from tales that began and disintegrated and began again and interwove and came back again to the beginning, while I tried to picture him as a younger man with a firmer jaw doing all that he said he had done.

But there we were in his garage room with his hands shaking from a nervous disorder and thoughts in my head to hold him and steady him and comfort him. And counter thoughts of shame. Of what would he think if he knew what I was thinking. Believing in his seriousness and goodness and knowing my foolishness and frivololity by comparison. Hearing his tales dwindle back to the typewriter on a makeshift desk, knowing that what he spoke of was no more. There had been a fire. He had lost his job. An executive position with Safeway Stores, advertising their soap, all kinds of soap. It was big business. He had been a big businessman with his own plane, trips to Puerto Vallarta. And he had married Faye, a Swedish woman with crooked teeth, who was overly self-conscious of her teeth. They had caused her to withdraw. They had deformed her lip. He encouraged he to believe in herself. He taught her to fly his airplane. He got her teeth straightened. She blossomed. Her voice took on an hysterical note. It was the sound of a once shy woman learning to swing. At forty she put on the smallest bathing suit she could find and went to the beach with a roll of fat hanging over the top of it, ignoring his protests and criticisms. He had given her too much confidence. She left him at home poking out business letters with one finger on his typewriter. She got a job as secretary to the headmaster of an expensive boys school. Everyone began responding to the way she believed in herself. Young professors wanted to take her out to dinner. She divorced Hank and made it known that she was tired of buying cigarettes and booze for him while he sat at his typewriter pretending he was still earning a living. She laughed at his study and called it a farce. We all heard her say at one time or another , "He's not going to sell any soap, ha, ha, ha."

The daughter's eyes were wide with fear. Her father had tried to strike her mother. They had hid behind locked doors from him. She got confused. She believed he wanted to hurt her too. The fear turned to hate. They escaped from him before Halloween. He had become a monster.

Now we stood around the interior of his empty rooms in our costumes. Ours for fun, his for real. He wore old clothes he had thrown on not in jest. They were wrinkled and mismatched not by choice. He attempted to look the way he used to when entering his Safeway Stores executive office. The social drink in his hand had turned to a self-prescribed medication. His shakes were D.T.s (delirium tremors from alcoholism).

We stood there in his haunted house. I with a gin and tonic, the children having already deposited whatever it was that he gave them, into their trick-or-treat bags. I heard their voices urging me to leave. They sensed something was not right. They saw the tremor of his hands. I stood, planted, a benumbed animal, knowing but not wanting to know. Wanting to run but staying, frozen as if by car lights at night. He came in close, staggering, and threw a heavy, water-logged arm around my shoulder and pulled my face to him while his mouth sought outward, sucking toward life. I held strong, supporting him and trying to turn away. We were like swimmers in a rough sea. My lips a buoy to him. He caught me somewhere on the face, mouth, cheek, chin, with his desperation. I felt wet flesh, softness and hardness. And tasted the saline solution of saliva. He stepped back and looked at my face, his target, to get better aim, keeping one hand on my shoulder, positioning me. The children were making little sounds of urgency to leave.

Gaiety resounded from my throat and I stepped away, smiling, chortling about going to other houses so the children could get more and more candy, ignoring his attempt to hold on, letting him sink below the surface. I glanced back as we pushed toward the door and saw him trying to steady himself, bewildered.

He died within two years. His shaky hands finally stilled. His grizzled lips sealed. His typewriter in a secondhand store along with the business books. Boxes of his special formula soap, his latest invention, sitting around in the way. It was a soap that would be slow to soften but quick to lather. A soap with an irresistible scent.

And curses still coming from the mouth of a woman he tried to help and then tried to violate when she no longer needed his help. When he needed hers.

I always want to tell him that I noticed his predicament when I think of him. When I remember his wet drowning mouth.

THE GRAPH IN THE SKY

On the graph in the sky. Ed and I stand at the polo field and draw verbal lines from this square to that showing where our lives are going and have been, charting out the courses of them from the time when we knew each other back in high school. He has hair thickness starting high and ebbing down toward the bottom of the page to someday baldness. While his jogging ability starts at zero and moves in a never faltering upward line, never plateauing. Not yet. Going up and off the page. I pencil in aging skin the way he does thickness of hair. Spiraling down. But it sharply crosses the strong upward line of jogging faster and longer and neither one level off. Yet. Either. And we try to get each other to understand how it is possible to hold even by replacing what is taken with abilities in other areas. And we call it improved cardio-vascular systems. We stand together with our balding head and withering face and talk of how we are trading youth for the stronger cardio-vascular system. And we pass the few minutes cooling off that way, breathing deep after two miles in fourteen minutes.

7.

I Go For A Walk shows her very close to how she functions as a physical creature.

A Scene: I Go for a Walk

I go for a walk and one leg becomes the pillar for the other one to skitter around. I am surprised how the body balances itself out, and that I am not crippled. One leg plants itself, in a second, and the other one pushes off from it in another second, and I walk all the way up to Mark's grapes that way. Plant, push, plant, push, etc.

Mrs. Henson drives by with her pink fat daughter beside her in whom she keeps virginity. She hauls around the great mound of virgin flesh, safely preserved, and stops to pick up the lead, homely younger daughter who sleeps with a hippie. The neighborhood knows how Mrs. Henson had her phone changed to an unlisted number trying to prolong the younger daughter's virginity. How the daughter's eyes were red from crying back then. And how Mrs. Henson could not look anybody in the eye for awhile when the Volkswagen bus appeared before her house and was always parked there with a long-haired man sitting in it and her younger daughter sitting out there with him 'till all hours until we all accepted it as a fixture and lost interest in smirking. And how the daughter began to look less homely and no longer had red eyes.

Mrs. Henson smiles at me as they pass. It is the first time I have seen her smile since her younger daughter grew up. She is accepting it. And she is happy now carting around the compromises. She has the fat virgin beside her as the package of all she ever believed in. And the thin one is there too.

I pass aunt Martha's house. She is the old maid who goes off to Mexico once a year and comes back flushed. The house is cottage-like and the garden is squared off with the bushes and shrubs organized into patterns to show her control over them. She lives with an old and shy bachelor brother, and a mother who is packed away in a back bedroom and who comes out only when she hears the sound of the piano. It is the old woman's cue. The neighborhood has heard rumors that she used to be a concert pianist. Neighborhood children are frightened when they visit and bang on the piano and the old woman comes out and looks at them, staring hard, as if trying to remember what the sound means to her.

I reach Mark's grapes. They are the large green ones with the light, strange taste to them. They grow by the roadside on a fence, and no one picks them. Mark grows them for foliage on the old wooden fence. I pick all I can carry on my left arm when I fold it across my waist. And because all the weight is to the left, my feet devise a new rhythm as I walk back home again.

7.

As Guests is about pretentiousness in front of the elderly, and then back to the coarseness of herself.

As Guests

Down the block: (We are so well-mannered and I can write forever and there are so many promises of good things to come.) While we chat with Betty and Clara, (The responsibility of) our lives vanish. We sit and sip martinis in the tropical room of these two old German sisters. The good life surrounds us and we believe in our humble efforts off in the distance, a block away, as enlightened effort. We are good. All is good. There is no way to superimpose our other sides onto this clean scene in the Bovabecks house. We believe we do not have genitals or palates or entrails. Our hands fold and unfold like those of a preacher. Our nails are clean and polished. They have never been dirty. We do not know what toe jam is, have never heard of it. Would never think of such a thing. We speak in sweet positives. Smiling. Saying things that will not defile these sweet old ladies. Will not shock them. An atrocity is mentioned, the flood, the poor Mexicans a mile away were washed out of their shacks. We frown as if the thought is too strong, too evil, too terrible to accept: how could there be such a thing in "life." As if we have never dragged ourselves through sludge and muck ourselves, as if they have never come over from Germany to a better life in America, clutching at pennies until they could afford not to. As if Alex and I never packed his old truck full of our collective junk and made our way toward hope and promise fifteen years before.

We talk and chit chat and sip for four hours. We never get near the things that are going on: Clara's heart trouble, their widowism, their loneliness, their fear of dying, or theft, of insanity. We never talk about the hate we have for certain things. We talk about their rubber plants, their cat, their trip to New York, the restaurant business which made them rich, the heart attacks their German husbands had under the strain of owning their own restaurants. We marvel over cholesterol, the wind, the rain, the peacocks and guinea hens that visit their yard. Good Viennese waltzes play on their stereo phonograph. They smile at us, believing in our goodness. A young couple. They castrate us with what they think we are. Soon it is time to go home.

The refinement wears off very slowly as we enter our own house. We try to maintain the self-discipline, the sitting properly, the placing of the feet just so, the knees together. We want to continue being company, guests, well-mannered visitors *in* our own *life*. But the demands of our own place nag us. Require the legs to come apart, hands to unfold. Out of sight of the old ladies we become loud, coarse, moving fast and violently, getting something done, cursing if it doesn't go right. We have passion. We do not forget we can escape through sex. Can arrange things by force. We holler, demand, command. Impulse ticks away. The groin pulsates. We are home.

8.

A Dream shows two parts of herself, at odds,
the young colt and an old cow.

A Dream

A rope is tied to a horse and a cow. The horse is climbing a
wall, trying to get away. It is a young stallion. The old cow
is being tugged at, jerked, made to bawl. A whole town,
or a school, is the audience. I am in charge of the stallion.
Everyone knows it and knows it is causing a fuss, out of
control, a problem…. They are tolerant, biding time. Their
silent waiting is unspoken criticism. I pretend indifference.
Alex is somewhere "knowing" all this, trying not to be embarrassed. He is near our house, which has been completed
with a deep, dark, rich, impressive entrance. The front tree
is curling forward just exactly as it should if it had been
landscaped. And I am on a barren knoll away from him
with the horse, a cow out of control.

As a family: We want to do something as a family. That
means Alex will not sink into a science magazine or motor
manual, or I will not pick up a New Yorker. Or we will not go
pour a glass of wine, or disappear into a bedroom. As a family
means we can go swim at the Y, go bowling, go to a movie, go
to the shopping center and look at all the things we could have
or already have or don't want to have. We could go eat, go visit
another family, go to the snow, go for a walk, a drive, a sailboat
ride. While we think about it, the day drifts away, Alex goes out
on the front porch to see the night fall, the wind blow, the rain

come down, to pick up the newspaper. He comes in carrying a potato bug by one of its spiney legs, announcing his find, tying the family together in instant interest. He drops it in the rat cage and as a family we watch the rat chew off its head. The crunching sound gives me indigestion. I throw up in the bathroom, but still cannot get rid of the feel of scraping prickly bug legs in my throat. I fall asleep on the couch and wake up with chills. There is laughter as a family in front of the television set. All the things to do fall away as the hour grows late. We do nothing, stay home, in unison we have wanted to do something as a family.

The Fictional Meeting-of-the-Future

She went to the refrigerator and opened three different dark bottles and took out two vitamins from each one and put them all in her mouth and drank them down with sips of lemonade. And thought about seeing him across the room sometime at a nice place and looking radiant again, and going over to him and being gracious. No matter who he was with. But she imagined him alone. Without a partner because it was the only way she had ever seen him. Leaning, drinking a vodka drink. Brooding. Looking full of thought. Her skin would be scented and full. She would be fresh and new. Even though it would be a few years from now. He would have matured and taken on the anxiety of nearing his late twenties. It would be good to see that in him.

And then she carried the bag of wine and things from the night's efforts before and she thought about how they had told each other things they had never wanted to tell each other in the beginning. Honest things. "It was never love. It was something else all along" – type of thing. Or, "I loved you in a way you will never understand, in a way you failed to grasp" – type of thing. And she held the brown paper bag with both hands. It was heavy and she held it like an old Indian carrying a bundle of twigs that is too big and too heavy. Round shouldered. Clutching hands. Contorted face in fear of not being able to carry it much longer. She went away from their friendship in that manner, hunching and old. And took the night before's efforts into the house and put them away. Put him away until that fictional meeting of the future.

9.

Out There: Her parakeet showed her this about herself: The cage door was left open and it didn't fly away. It knew instinctively that there were dangers and its wings were unpracticed and weak.

Out There

Mildred was scaring herself again reading the want ads and apartment rentals. They had been not really fighting but soured on each other for some time again. Life ahead looked like a stretch of barren land when a phase like this hit them. It was an emotional blight. They could not open their mouths to each other without the words withering their hearts into dried stubble. She spent about an hour reading alternatives in her little corner chair and getting a glimpse of herself in a new life *out there*, as a dental assistant, or a hostess at Holiday Inn, or a trainee at Applied Magnetics. She saw herself leading people to dentist chairs and snapping on paper bibs or showing them to tables and handing out menus or working with tweezers and miniature electronic parts under magnifying glass and she knew how she'd be inside – like a gigantic awkward water creature on dry land. Not believing in any of it. It going nowhere.

She could not do anything except teach grammar school and there was no work for an older teacher who qualified for a salary in the second column. Only new first year teachers were being hired because they were cheap. Old teachers hung on to their jobs with chiton-like grips called tenure.

Mildred had traipsed home from her teaching career years before to raise a family. Home to stay. Mildred always underwent a chilling on the inside when she read about the possibilities of escaping her present life and flitting out into an unfamiliar future. She always imagined a faceless male appearing at the door of her new apartment ready to kill her. A bad man who had watched her efforts at freedom with extra-sensory vision and saw into her dilemma and knew of her helplessness against his evil plans. Maybe it was guilt that made her envision this form of punishment. Punishment, always in the form of a man.

Guilt, that she should try to break away instead of staying and being an enduring heroine. Guilt, that she should think of herself and want to attempt a life of her own rather than die a slow death next to a husband in the long tedious plan they had made years before.

She put the paper down and basked in the relief that she was still *here* and not *out there* yet. Her home held her safe in its familiarity and the sourness faded a little from the man who had said hateful things to her over the years. What were hateful things after all compared to the *unknown*. She swung back into the routine of pressing a mound of ground beer into a skillet until it crumbled into the makings for tacos. Probably her thousandth pan of tacos over the years. But what was a thousand tacos against a barren tacoless kitchenette in some dilapidated apartment building that she had yet to find.

Money. If she could just get enough money she could go away from all of the *old* into all of the *new*. She could avoid drooping in the doorway of the employment bureau with spaniel eyes begging for a scrap of job. She could avoid viewing the cheapest apartments and seeing the scum of past tenants dripping from and stuck to the sinks and toilets. She could avoid the smell of musty rugs and walls. She could avoid going from her life into an older life. What was her fresh little home, even if it had become a prison, against the staleness *out there* of the only things she would be able to afford.

She had thought of running her own ad in the want ads. It would say:

WANTED: NEW SITUATION.
JESUS TYPES WITH BIG WALLETS
AND DESIRE TO SAVE SINKING SOUL
APPLY P.O. BOX ......

Hope was always in the form of a male.

They told her it was like learning to swim. You jump in and the motions are learned after you are in the water. You jump in and there's "somebody" to catch you and hold you up from sinking until you've mastered the strokes. She had stood in a pool for six weeks once and urged her tiny tots, playfully named the Tadpoles by YMCA, to jump. Come on, jump. Mommy will catch you. And they did and she did and they learned to swim better than she ever could. Her mommy had never stood in a pool and promised to catch her. She learned to swim in the ocean at sixteen, battered by the waves. She never learned to dive head first.

Now the newspaper urged her and her instinct urged her and the world *out there* urged her to jump in. But she balanced on the solid form of her old life and could not jump. She teetered, hesitating, holding back and would not jump for fear that "they" might not be reliable. "They," her resources. She did not trust her resources anymore. She knew how she could get. How she could close everything out and move around in the mysterious weird underwater world of her emotions and almost drown. The most important movement of all, that of a positive response to the currents around her, quick talk, laughter, bullshit, she had lost. And that was what would keep her buoyed. Fear gripped her now. She would sink unless she could remember how to believe in lively chatter, senseless laughter, and meaningless carrying on with people after being solemn and cynical in her hide-out over the years.

She went about crumbling ground beef and wondering if she could ever make a leap. Her heart leapt at a sudden thought that someone might sneak up behind her and give her a push.

10.

A Small Way: a glimpse of starting over and getting it right this time.

A Small Way

Something has told her: *Start over*. Start fresh. She thinks it has been telling her that for a long time, but it is the first time she has heard it. It is the first time she wanted to listen. For an answer that she didn't know she was asking. She thinks it is a question she has been asking for a long time but didn't know she was asking it: What should I do? Start over. Start fresh.

In her small way she began. She took out a bottle of Pine Sol and wiped down all the surfaces that surrounded her. She took off all that had accumulated on top of all the surfaces and got the surfaces down bare. But still it was not enough and the thing said: Start over. It seemed to hiss in her ears. Begin fresh. So she went out to the garage and stood looking at the cans of paint, reading their labels: Eggshell, Ochre, Beige, Champagne, Sandstone, Ivory ... She caught herself standing there reading the labels. And in her small way she was astonished. She was not going to paint. Not today. Not tomorrow. Maybe someday again, but not soon. She hated the mess. But she could not leave the garage for all the gazing and contemplating she was doing over the names of brand new colors, imagining them over all the old surfaces, fresh, clean. She tore herself away and went directly to the car.

She found herself walking down the aisle of cleaning fluids, powders, sprays. She caught herself lifting bottles of Windex,

Oven-Off, Clorox, BonAmi. She studied the chick by the cracked egg shell and read, perplexed, Hasn't Scratched Yet. She grabbed a new bottle of Pine Sol, and searched the other products for what they did, reading the instructions as if they could be answers. Lysol, Hexol, Phenol, Drano, Airwick, lemon oil, Boroteem… They flashed in her mind like neons: START OVER. Begin again.

On the way home a flock of small brown birds flew from where they were feeding in a plowed field and crashed into her car. She blinked and dodged as they hit the windshield and her foot touched the brake but she didn't stop because it was too late. In the mirror she saw three fall in the street and her stomach clenched tight. Birds knew how to dodge cars. That had never happened to her before. Was something trying to stop her from going forward? She arrived home with all the cleaning agents and went about digging out rags, tearing sizes, filling pots with hot water, diluting preparations and attacking places that hadn't been touched for a long time. After awhile she began to feel relief. Her hands were stained, fingernails encrusted. Dust had collected in her hair, dirt on her clothes. The front of her shirt was smudged at the belly and breasts like a baby's bib. Sweat stood out on her face and trickled down her scalp and arm pits. And she rested, standing in the middle of her house staring at nothing.

Start over hissed at her again. Begin new. She put down the rags and went outside to get away from it. She had gone over everything. In her small way a word formed on her lips: *How?*

11.

Scanning The Surface: Looking around the inside of the life she's created and seeing an absence of reward.

Scanning the Surface

It was quiet in the house. No one else was up. There was something about creeping around on the surface of her life while everyone slept. There was something about not being bothered by demands, needs, requests. She had awakened on the couch with an aching back earlier than usual; the couch where she had taken to falling asleep like an old man after he has taken his evening meal. In an old hotel. Her plate of chicken bones and oily lettuce remains were still on the table beside the couch. She did not like seeing it. The stagnation of it. The no-progress of it. It should have been moved along up into the next day toward a goal: into a cupboard, clean, ready to use again. And she, herself, should have creamed and washed her face and brushed he teeth and exercised her limbs and torso. If rot was beginning on her plate, it was beginning in her mouth and in her body. She and her whole life had been moving along like the cycle of the dishes until now. And now she fell asleep in the middle of an act of duty to the kitchen and to herself. She was beginning to rot. It scared her.

   She could not get the belief back. That it was vital to go through the motions and *do everything that was supposed to be done.* The belief was not gone. It was there, ingrained, so that she felt guilt and panic rising, but she did not listen to it anymore. Perhaps she believed in it too much and was holding out from it like a child saying no to big mama with a stick over a rule that must be obeyed. No, I won't do any of it any more. No, I don't care if it's good for me or not. No, no, no. Because, look. I've been doing it for thirty-six years and where am I? Here? No, no, no. And Wap. Take that: rotten teeth. Another Wap: a roll of fat on the gut. And Wap again: a big loose ass and saggy breasts. The stick strikes and she protests. Wap: crows feet, jowls, over-hanging upper eyelids and bags, a mouth with a line to the chin like a puppet. Wap. Wap. Wap....

But she's tough. She remains rigid. She does not give in to mama who wants her to do what's good for her when she can see it's not good for her. And anybody can see it. So she falls asleep after dinner and lets time stop. And the rot begin. The Waps. She taunts deterioration and eggs it on, hysteria pecking away in her throat. Com'on, if decay is the game, if it's threatening she'll threaten back. And she doesn't brush her teeth like a good girl, or do sit-ups, or clean the pores of her face or think positively. She drinks a glass of wine and smokes an experimental cigarette and skitters around like the child with a piece of candy when mama wants her to eat her green beans. Com' on, she dares it to destroy her... Ha, ha, ha.

She is sick about it and confused. It is beyond her. It comes from a part of her she cannot control. This part makes her into a brat. It embarrasses her. And humiliates her. She has always been *sensible*. Always. Sensible. Before, when she thought it would pay off. She sees the pay-off now every time she goes to the mirror, every time she goes to her purse. She sees what big people told her would happen if she were bad. You'll be ugly, you'll be poor. So she wasn't bad. She looks in the mirror and in her purse and she hasn't even been bad. Yet.

12.

The Big Male Dog: Seeing her dog as an equal in the scheme of things, not pulling rank as a human.

The Big Male Dog

The big male. Dog. I have already taken him in to have a vasectomy. And brought him home. If I had taken my husband in to have one he would not be lying around on the floor licking the stitches along the underside of his penis where the incision was made to get at the vas deferens. But the big male. Dog. Does. Lap, lap, lap. All day until I hurt and feel squeamish all over. Once I heard a slight pop, as his teeth tugged at a stitch. And I say, no, you'll spill yourself, don't. And he gave an impression of apology, a hint of wag in the tail, a series of swallowings, a glance up with lowered head. I leaned down and carefully held his back leg up to see the long pink seam and something in me squirmed and tried to run. He let me look. There was no modesty in him. What existed, existed. One part being no more important than another. And no less. I tried to make the operation up to him by giving him all the leftovers in the refrigerator. I piled them on a paper plate next to his heaping bowl of untouched kibble. Wienies and pork and beans, grated cheese, cold tacos, a chicken back. Some green squash with clumps of cold butter clinging to it. He walked gingerly. To the dish and chose selectively. Piece by piece until it was gone and the plate was clean. After that we went for a walk.

The big male. Dog. And me. Me, with a rope around his

neck. He, with stitches. He with a mental rope around my neck. Me with mental stitches. We go along together, respecting each other. Symbiotic friends. I wish to deny him no pleasure. And he wishes to do me no harm, in fact, to protect me. I have not castrated him. He marks territory up and down the street, eager, after the anesthetic, to reclaim a part of the world. I squint in the sun and pretend there is not all that much importance going on at the end of the leash in my hand. We make our way like big male. Dog. And a female back to the house, to my territory, where the lapping begins again.

Once he tried to hold me like a baby and I wanted to get up. I felt like a cow down in the winter. I said, "But I'm a mother. *I* hold. *I am not* held.*" I could not take it. My face became a grotesque mask under his eyes. My body was solid bone and freckle. It did not go into contours and fit against him. So we traded positions. And I felt better holding him. Except I could not be tender. I thought he would think, "Oh, yeah. A Head against her breast, any head and she brushes back the hair. It's a routine. There is nothing else to do to a head against your breast." But he didn't think it. He couldn't. It wasn't in him. He believed* his *head was the only head. And he never went beyond that. I learned later.*

I awake in the sun on the deck. The blue sky is blue against my eye. Salt stings my eyes and I close them again. It is the only way I know there is sweat on my face. The sting of salt as it runs into my eyes. A bold leaf is in the blue of the sky in front of my eyes. It is a leaf extended across the yard on a branch. An avocado leaf. From an avocado branch. And it stands thick and leathery above my eye against the sky. A coarse forceful green against almost no blue. I raise one arm to shade my eyes and my hand hovers above me on an arm. A brown flesh arm. Mine. With a joint that allows it to be raised. Above my eyes. The sky, the leaf, my arm. Things are registering. Sight things.

13.

What Was: Looking back.

What Was

She sees an old man watching her and she knows what he wants. He watches her with young man memories in his eyes. She sits caved-in trying to be unhealthy. Trying to experience unhealthiness. In Thrifty. While a little boy gets a doughnut. A timeless pleasure. And two plump Mexican women order two ham sandwiches as if they weren't Indians once, hunting boar with bow and arrow.

She waits for a guy who killed himself. Not because it would be good anymore between them, but because he killed himself when they still loved each other. She looks up and sees that the old man has disappeared. She is sorry. She wanted to give him something. She creates an environment in the vinyl booth. Starving her lungs of oxygen, listening to Musak, pretending to be alone. Pretending it's *all over*. Pretending she has *nothing left*. It leaves her free to wallow in *what was*. Her personal history. The way she fought ether at four and sodium pentathol at twenty-four. And again at thirty-four. Nothing entered her body at fourteen. The way a boy once said WOW when he saw her face, and after a man did irrational things in order to be near her. A bit of glory she keeps tucked away. To keep going.

There were *some times*. A few times that come back to her when she wants something. On a cool sheet. In summer. Without words. Maybe sighs. And *somebody* there. Their arms around each other. Not in the spotlight. Never in cap and gown.

Only on a cool sheet, sighing. Those are *the times*. That come back. If she could get anything to reoccur. Those would be the times.

She regards her lungs as two little people and wants to explain to them to give her time, that she is just fooling around. She means them no harm. There are certain indulgences she would never take. Mostly with food. She would never buy a dish of six strawberries featured in the Thrifty refrigerated shelf, for instance. Never.

She sees someone fighting to get the experimental cigarettes away from her, knocking them out of her hands to save her. Growing cold and sick as she inhales. And light as a feather and padded in cotton. Angry with everyone so she can be alone. Severed. Floating. A wisp. Not really there. Only knowing about being there. Her shoulders are sore from digging in the yard. Because it is spring. There is something about the soil in the spring. While he is buried in a yard. Somewhere in Chicago. He will not come in through the door and sit across from her. Anymore. She captured earthworms and put them in a jar to show to all the children that come to her *what an earthworm is*. While earthworms crawl in and out of him in Chicago. Chicago earthworms.

When she glances around she sees that all the people look like another country. She does not know the frowsy young men who cannot mess their hair up enough to show that they have powerful feelings and thoughts. She decides when she goes home that she will unplug the clock.

14.

She Could Say Look: to people, wondering
why she never was "bad" and tried to smoke.

She Could Say Look to People

She liked to contend with a cigarette. She liked the feel of it.
To be ever vigilant of the burning end. To watch that it didn't
burn her or that she didn't burn anything with it. To worry
about running out of cigarettes. It was a new concern. And to
remember to pick some up when she dashed out on an errand.
It was a new concept. It was the way she had seen other people
doing it for years.

And best of all was the problem of health. She could
fret and talk about being afraid of dying of lung cancer. And
emphysema. She could hurt herself and worry about hurting
herself and get other people to worry about it too. She could
light up the end of a filtered cigarette and worry about all the
damage such a simple pleasure would cause.

She could look nervous. The way she had seen other
people looking nervous. As if she had a serious problem. And
needed to smoke. Silently, desperately, dramatically, tragically.
Demonstrating her anxiety. Puffing and blowing and creating a
cloud of mystery and smoke around her head, constricting the
blood vessels of her brain, making her hands levitate. Or have
the sensation of the top of her head levitating. And her groin
turning to ice. And then when she had sucked the cigarette
down to the filter, she could search around for an ash tray and
spend some precious moments crushing out the ash, pressing

and squinting her eyes.

She could say *look* to people and hold a single piece of paper in trembling hands for them to turn casually and see how shattered her nerves were. They would think she was *high-strung*, words people said about skinny people who could not sit still, always fidgeted and looking unhappy. People who were going here and there wearing clothes that showed jutting elbows, lean shoulders, and boney knees. People who could not sleep and never went to bed early. People who went out into the dark of night to find something they couldn't find during the light of day.

She liked the squawking of her mother when she first lit a cigarette up in front of her. The alarm in the sixty year old eyes of a mother who had thought she got her daughter past all the dangers of growing up. And of the daughter saying, "I never had a choice not to smoke. I want to smoke and then choose not to. You chose for me."

She liked the absence of alarm in her father who had smoked all his life and separated himself from her that way. Men smoked. Women didn't. She sat at a table with him and insulted him by lighting up a cigarette. He denied her disapproval. His refusal to react was evidence of a strong reaction. He would not look surprised and feed her need to surprise him again and again. Even if there were not that many surprises left. Neither one of them were young. And when she tried to explain by saying, "I was too afraid not to. I wondered what was wrong with me that I never tried to smoke before. Not as a teenager or all through my twenties when everyone was doing it. I had to break through that." He just sat there smoking and knowing that she didn't know how to really smoke anyway.

15.

The Difference: Imagining smoking and then choosing not to, so that the decision was hers.

The Difference

I have a relationship with cigarettes. My father smoked from the very beginning of my life. I cannot picture him without cigarettes. It was part of the imprint. A man with a cigarette. A jaw line. A nose in profile with smoke coming out of it. Smoke all around the *male*. And the white small cigarette between his fingers. Busy fingers. Stained fingers. Nervous fingers. Capable fingers. Fingers that want to be everywhere, even where they shouldn't be. Maybe *especially* there. And there was something about a man who didn't smoke. He was lacking something.

I had an uncle who never smoked. He was like a boy scout. He never did anything that was not good for him. He never really grew up and went on to the American adulthood and did all the things minors cannot do: smoke, drink, swear, drink coffee, stay up late and fool around. He married an older woman and jogged on the beach and jumped rope with seaweed in the sand to build up his calves that were already like sharp rocks jutting beneath his olive colored flesh.

He never smoked. And when he showed up for my graduation ceremonies and the wedding he stood around smiling with idle hands, big and strong and kindly and healthy in a one hundred and sixty dollar suit. Back then that was expensive and my father wore a thirty dollar suit. While my father chain smoked and made everyone laugh with his jokes about the way everything was. His hands reached for and found cigarette packages and matches, his mouth and ash trays without his directing them the habit was so instilled. He coughed and twisted his neck to get the right feel in it, and he pinched off smiles of pride over his wit so that we would not see full nicotine stained teeth. When my uncle and father stood side by side they seemed to be having a contest to see who could spread their feet apart the furthest as if there was something about the stature of a man in the stance he could take. My uncle would chuckle gentlemanly and make a comment about my father's cigarette cough. But I could detect laughter in my father's eyes over my uncle's big puffed up wheat germ muscles and how he never used them for anything fun. How he had them just to have them. He never chased around. Women never saw them. Or stroked them.

My father was small and thin. But women stood around him and he made them giggle and feel like women.

I did not know about people like my uncle. I only understood people like my father who were determined to ruin their health. I knew why even though I couldn't do it myself. I knew that he wanted to feel things, pain and things. And I grew contemptuous of my uncle who spoke as if he had no genitals or bowels or teeth or fingernails. Or scar in the middle of his stomach where there was once an umbilical cord. A slimy organic cord bringing a bloody fluid into his slimy organic body. He would speak about rules: "Always wash the sand off your feet before you come into the house… This is the way to hold your knife and fork… Get a good education and nobody can take that away from you… exercise and fresh air and a healthful diet will do a world of good for anyone.…"

My father liked to hurt himself. He didn't believe in being comfortable. He would go without food and drink coffee until his heart would race and then come home and lie across the bed and worry about having a heart attack. He would drink coffee until his stomach would ache and burn and then talk about his anxiety over stomach cancer. My mother begged him to drink milk. He never got around to it. My uncle drank milk. Later my uncle *had* to drink milk because he developed a stomach ulcer. My father did not say it but I knew he felt triumphant when he heard about the ulcer. It meant that clean living did not pay off. He would glance at my uncle's big broad back and there would be the hint of a snicker in his eye. Later he would say something about his high pockets being up around his chest and how he would choke himself someday with his belt.

My father never went bald. His hair turned white and coarse but grew thick and full and looked as if it were blowing back in the wind. My uncle went bald on top. He began to take Geritol. My father increased his intake of cigarettes from two to three packs a day.

It was easy to entertain my father when he came to visit. I would serve coffee. When my uncle came I had to have juice and natural foods on hand. And milk. He would take Postum or Ovaltine sometimes. If we were all having coffee. It was as if my uncle was saving himself for something while my father wanted to be used up by the time he died. My uncle never stopped believing in all the things he believed in as a boy. While my father was trying to prove that none of it was true. Not love, not hard work, not health. None of it bringing happiness and success and wisdom. But love gone sour, and hard work not paying off, and health going old and tired. That bringing him closer to knowing what was going on. What he was all about.

Sometimes I wonder if the difference will be in the moment of death, if there is such a moment when they will evaluate their own particular lives. Will my uncle be confident that he did all the right things, while my father will be in doubt and tormented briefly wondering if he did anything right. Will that be the difference? The payoff for each style they led. Or will they both sum it up with the fleeting deathbed impression of *having done the best they knew how*, and die identical deaths, tired and glad it is over, trusting that *whatever* it is will understand them.

Will the only different be that the death rattle is louder in my uncle because his lungs were in better shape. I want to know because I have been saving myself like my uncle, but I have always wanted to use myself up like my father.

A Man's Stomach

It was a concept in my grandmother's mind. She said never to put pepper in it. It would irritate the lining. She took good care of her machine: my grandfather. It was the only machine she had.

16.

Out In The Big World: awkward at the great
age of thirty.

Out in the Big World

She felt like some old woman in a movie, stumbling up the
steps, dragging up in a gray rag dress, tattered and worn out by
pursuing duty.

She was climbing the stairs to the employment agency and
wearing a new short dress and hair cut and the young girl at the
desk respected her right off. Marty could tell by the response
she got even though she could not think of what to say to the
little secretary, at first.

She held out the newspaper ad section and used it as a
prop, pointing to the print and saying, "I wanted to ask about
your ads. There's one here for a copy typist." The words were
hard to find. She had not said copy typist, probably at all in her
life. She had only seen the words in books from time to time.
There had never been an opportunity to say it before this. She
had come from many years of being behind her stove and in
front of her sink where she had grown skillful swishing around
them with wordless thoughts which never reached her tongue.

The movements in her kitchen had become perfected.
She had gotten it down to a fine art. She had learned to waste
no motions over the years. There was no floundering around
toward the last years she'd spent there. Her body had developed a system which it carried out without direction from her
conscious thinking anymore. "Muscle memory" was an expres-
sion that would enter the vocabulary many years later. Her foot

stepped there and her hand shot out in that direction for the salt. It had been a dance. The dance of the housewife preparing a meal.

The girl explained the ads and then gave Marty an application form and left her. Marty sat down to fill it out. It slid off the inclined table onto the floor and the girl looked at Marty stooped over from her sitting position. Again she saw herself as a lean, gaunt old lady, squatting on a toilet, clumsy and with hands close to the floor, full of veins, bulging blue veins and knuckles. It was a surprise to her to see her own slim tan arm reach down and pick up the form.

Marty told the girl that she'd fill it out at home and would drop it off another time and then she left. She knew the secretary would look at her shoes as she walked out the door and at her legs, with those round blue eyes, young and critical, curious eyes about another predicament dropping by the office. Marty turned half way to catch the girl looking and to confirm it. She saw the resolve in the young face, never to be like that. Never to be creeping in somewhere, searching for a job. Because she had done that herself at twenty-two. She had looked at women of thirty-two with scorn and resolve and never with resignation.

Back in her car, Marty knew herself again. The face in the rear view mirror was the one she was used to. It looked ok. She was reassured. The refection of her in the employment window had been a stranger. A bare-legged stranger looking for a job. And asking a child for it.

She did not start the engine right away. There was no hurry now that she was alone. Out in the big world she could sit there awhile and take her time driving away. She thought about her home, the trails within it, worn by her own feet and how she had left it to go up the stairs of employment buildings, attempting to wear new trails somewhere else. She thought about the bed and the rugs. They filed past her mind's eye. The little children with their damp, frog-scented hands and smeared faces and disheveled heads. The fading image of the husband, the dominate male full of dominate male hormones. And then she Herself drifted by, full of recessive genes, causing a passivity to flow from her glands. It was the gift from all her recessive ancestors. Something passed on down the line so that walking up a stairway to ask for a job aged her ten years. She had a shy grandfather and a self-conscious grandmother, a meek great aunt and a reticent uncle, not to mention her own parents. No one had been dominate.

The moving picture continued and she saw her husband and herself living side by side for years. She was crying some- times and getting into her car sometimes with her suitcases and looking always for his approval. The film got hung up (in her mental projector) and one picture stuck. It became a single still photograph and she saw them, ten years of them in one glossy print. And the reel was over. It no longer moved.

She had gotten into her car for the last time and had driven away for the last time to wherever she had been wanting to go. Marty looked at the name on the front of the employment bureau. Her pots and pans, just handling them, would be a massage. She knew each handle. She had gotten to the point of finding them in the dark and she wished they were on the car seat beside her.

As she had driven away from them that last time she looked back and listened for machine gun shots or for any kind of ret- ribution. Tearing away would be a still shot of herself in action. She would always be in a perpetual state of fleeing, and looking back to see who was after her.

She drove away from her parking place and headed for the library. It was a home away from home. It had a bathroom, and a place to fill out the application form.

She parked and went into the big quiet room and followed a tremendous sized girl into the tiled restrooms. The girl turned and caught Marty looking at her back. Marty averted her eyes and went directly into a booth to hide. She hung up her purse and did not spread a sanitary paper on the seat of the toilet because she believed people who read books did not get syphilis, and wondered if it would be possible to wear paths in public places in order to feel comfortable again, out here where she had run to with her suitcase.

A merry tinkle came from the booth next to hers. She could see the large feet from under the wall between them. The sound was the same as her own. And it was out here where she had always wanted to be, in the big world. When the big girl left, Marty came out and wondered if she would ever be able to get her random movements down to a fine art again, as she washed her hands and turned the faucet handle the wrong way.

17.

A Bad Man Will Never Come: from the outside, they were always in the house.

A Bad Man Will Never Come

I am sitting in the front room sipping coffee and listening to music which reminds me of myself because I have heard it many times while I was doing the things I have to do. I want to get up and turn it off so I won't have to think of all the things I did and the way I keep doing them over and over again.

A thud sounds on the roof and there is a thud inside my chest in response. I hear the children calling in fright from their bedrooms, "What is that noise?"

I go in and say, "Be quiet. It's nothing. Just the cat jumping around probably."

"I'm afraid," they say in voices that register fear, high and frail, unprepared to defend themselves. I wonder where all the animals in us have fled to as I turn on the outside light and press myself against the window in full view of the bad man if there is one.

I don't believe in bad men. So I stand there awhile and look. The cat is stalking and looking up at me. I know a bad man will never come. He will never do atrocious things at my house because I don't believe in him. I imagine him coming. I see him peering in at me and warm ripples crawl up my head. I see him feeling for a crack in my house which will allow him to enter. And I know how I'll approach him, as one fellow human to another, not as a victim. I'll say, "Hi, how come you want to be like this. We all have reason to. You're not alone. It's just that the rest of us control ourselves. Let's talk and get to an understanding. You don't have to go around being bad. It's ludicrous to come in and hurt me or take something or whatever you're planning to do. You could be doing something else. Something constructive."

I hear my children saying, "Lock all the doors, Mommie." I don't like locking doors. It attracts bad men to lock doors. I don't want to drag through an evening fearing accidental death, until my face hangs. But for the children I go from door to door and as the locks click into place there are clicks of fear in my heart and I know why I never go around clicking locks routinely every night.

Smoke came out of only one of his nostrils. And his face was always warm. His circulation was close to the surface. But when he was dead his body was a trunk. His arms limbs. Like on a monkey. They were no longer his after they were lifeless. They belonged to the animal world. Dead limbs, a dead torso. No longer him. Physical evidence that he had been here once. But not him.

18.

I See Chimpanzees Nibbling: Longing to nibble and never again, sit down to eat, after years of family dinners.

I See Chimpanzees Nibbling

I sit on the bus bench and wait for my ride, not the bus but my husband who is coming to pick me up. I watch the entrance of the Chinese store across the street where a young man comes out holding a submarine sandwich and is peeling back the paper, preparing to eat it.

That is what I want. I immediately know it. I know it as soon as I see him. I know that all my life that is all I ever wanted food to be, a thing you do on your way to something else.

I want to be that man walking along the sidewalk eating his dinner on his way to what he really wants to do. I want to eat a sandwich while I drive over to a friend's house. I want a submarine sandwich on my desk and one beside my book on the deck. I want a sandwich in the bathroom and one on the beach and one in my car and one beside my bed on the bedstand. I never again want something in a plate and a plate on a table and a table in a room and the room for eating in.

I see chimpanzees nibbling all day long while they do other things. I see them snatching and chewing leaves while they copulate, play, travel and pick one another. And I see myself without a family eating something so wet that it drips and runs down my chin so that I have to lean over and let it spatter on the sidewalk.

My husband drives up and I get in, looking out my window at

the man with the end of his submarine sandwich in his mouth. We pass him. I say to my husband, "Wouldn't it be nice not to make a big deal out of food."

He says, "Speaking of food, I hope we have some of those good hot biscuits for dinner."

19.

The Permanent Wave: Seeing a stranger in the mirror of the beauty shop, after knowing herself only in the mirrors in her house.

The Permanent Wave

In the Coif Room there is a woman nearing her middle thirties who has not been to a beauty shop before because she did not think she needed one. She has passed by beauty shops before, though, on her way to sensible things. And she has glanced in their windows and smirked at women sitting in chairs with their hair at different stages of preparation, knowing they believed there would be a change when their hair was finished. A change that would lift them above their ordinariness.

She had felt sadness as she smirked. Sadness because nothing would change the women and she had smirked over that part of them that kept on believing it could happen. The everlasting ray of hope that would follow them to their deaths.

At thirty-four she had made an appointment, herself, half smirking, half sad, but straining toward the possibility, any small chance, that maybe it could make a difference. That perhaps, all those women weren't wrong, after all, and that she had been mistaken all these years about beauty shops.

She faced her face for four hours and did not know the face that was Her. She did not know the woman who sat looking back at her from the large stark, clear mirror. It was a woman with an aging face that crinkled up like any other face she had seen anywhere.

"A permanent. I just want body. Not a lot of curl. Just thicker hair," she told Nicholas. And she knew she was saying

"Make me into myself again. Give me back my identity."

The woman who watched her from the mirror all morning looked like all those women she had seen on the street all her life. Brown haired housewives, clutching at their purses and at their lives so they could get bargains. Women who had been given just enough to get by on, but not an ounce more, not an ample supply of anything.

She saw a kind of averageness studying her face as she studied herself in the mirror periodically, glancing and then looking away, down at the two veined hands in her lap. They were hands that went with the face. Hands that belonged to all those women she had seen all her life on streets and in little houses. The women who clutched at things, like carpeting and fabrics for draperies late in life, in their thirties, because it took them that long to get them.

She could not look at herself after awhile, so she took up a Cosmopolitan magazine and tried not to study the flawlessness of the models as she turned to an article about living off your beauty, called "sleeping for riches." She read, eager to undo the image and find superficiality in the women who could get by that way. She held each derogatory fact tightly in order to crack their perfection, as she would a nut.

The beautiful women stared up at her from the pages, from everywhere, Tampax ads, shampoo, bath oils, fashion, lovely faces smirking at her attempt, at her hope, as she had smirked in her twenties at women in their thirties. And she tried to see herself in the great light of IF. "If" loomed in and relieved her, somewhat, as she thought, "If I'd had all the………that they'd had, then……."

But she could not lie. At the end of the morning, as she surveyed her hair from the back with a hand mirror, she knew what she was. The permanent had been permanent. It had broken a pact she had thought she had with a part of herself. A pact that said she was different and would be protected from all those things that happened to other people. They would not happen to her. And here she was with somebody else's face. Where had her individuality gone? Where had She gone? When did she begin to look like the role she had to play instead of the person she had believed she was?

As she prepared to leave she took one last glance at the face in the beauty shop mirror. The face she had never seen before. Not at home. Not reflected in anybody's glasses, in store windows, in hubcaps, toasters, or rear-view mirrors.

And Nicholas fondled her coif, as he was paid to do, and told her things he told all the women. As she paid him, she wanted to go home and stand under the shower and wash it all away. She wanted to take off her dress-up clothes and put on her old bag work clothes and bend over a field somewhere and find solace from becoming like everyone else. She felt ashamed of all the costumes she had ever worn and all the thinking of being unique she had ever done. She wanted to hide because she was embarrassed by it happening to her, too. An old face just as it happens to anyone, just anyone.

The old man at the parking lot said, "Thank you ma'am," as she gave him her parking ticket to stamp, and drove away.

All night I pictured him watching me as I sat in my chair or wandered from room to room. It was raining and even though I knew he would not be standing out in the rain just to watch me moving about in my house, just to see me, *I could not let up on his audience. It was what I wanted.*

Later he became a tiny silver sliver. A metal shaving in my life. Slipped in without my knowing it, even though I knew I was playing around with metal. I find him there and am alarmed but relieved to know the source of my discomfort. I can remove him, but not without some pain.

At the park some kids come down for a picnic and stand around eating their sandwiches wondering why it is not fun. They believed all they had to do was have a picnic. *They do not understand yet about the spirit of the thing.* That *it requires more than* sandwiches in a park.

What is it in an old female that loses playfulness. Children romp and she will not join them. She does not think of herself as a full and heavy female yet, who cannot romp. But even he *treats her as the* old female *who* must be left alone. *"Don't play with her," is in* his *puppy eyes when he nips in and teases just to jump back and dodge her claws. He laughs. She lays, grouchy.*

20.

The Cat Show: People in public again, and traces of aging.

The Cat Show

We're all in rows with our cats in cages, waiting to have them inspected. It is not my idea. It is a child's. So we sit and wait and comb the cat. The competition is Household Pet. It is nothing special. It is an experience in *Cat Show*. For her.

Cat lovers mill around, looking at one another's cats. They are lovers of the exotic, wearing costumes, make-up and hair-dos and believing cats are more than they are. Or believing in as much as a cat can be. One woman's big rear is shining out in the health of her big red cheeks. A hippie goes by saying to himself, "Yeah, man, this is alright," as if his discovering it, us all there with our cats, originated us instantaneously, and his approval made it good. Like God.

Balls of cat fur skitter like live mice across the floor. And Prunella comes by, arms folded, widowism written on her face and in her manner. Thick pink lipstick that hasn't been smeared by a man for five years. Her second virginity held tight until a man somewhere, someday, can win it away from her.

A little girl overhears her elders talking about cats shedding. Wherever she goes she hears the word "shedding." Finally she asks her mother what is so bad about shedding and no one answers her. For two days no one ever answers her question about shedding. She does not understand about hair getting in the mouth yet. Someday the question about shedding will be answered for her without words.

The teenage son of the people next to us comes in obediently and passively to the cat show and sits all day with his little sister. The mother and father look alike and sit there side by side. They are meek people. Perhaps they were cousins once that got married, married each other because they were afraid of everyone else. The son has the same look. He is meek, but on his face are violent eruptions, nasty, wild, vulgar, primitive pimples, full of the hormones he represses from emerging elsewhere.

On the other side of us are the people, a family, who will take home all the ribbons. Their cat lays sluggish and gigantic inside their cage. They pet it and talk to it and it ignores them. It cannot be aloof enough. I want to starve it and leave it out in the rain in order to teach it about *life*. But I sit in front of my own cage and talk unnaturally to my own cat, the cat that lives outside and is not allowed inside the house because I do not like fur all over the place. The cat that gets dried kibble on the front porch, and now receives, in front of all the people at the cat show, moist canned fish.

The family with the future champion are not playing around. When life is over for them they will be able to say, "We had a cat *well*." It is how middle class Americans have a cat. Having it means spaying, grooming, feeding properly. It is a good lesson in cat care for their children. But not a lesson in *reality*. That would mean something else. My eyes move closer together with the smugness I feel in my private knowledge of reality. *Suffer* moves big in my mind.

This family will never learn about cats. They will only learn about how to pity less fortunate cats and to admire more fortunate breeding. Their cat has become The Standard, and all cats have become relative to it. They believe that what they do is what should be done. And they do it without perspective so they will never know their own definitions. They believe they are the way people and cats are supposed to be.

Familiar faces come by and smile and peer into our cage

and see plain old Rags. She is calico, black and orange and white so we have ingeniously decorated the cage to camouflage her. They have to peer at length to catch a glimpse of her. "Oh," they say and then go away on to other cages and bigger and better cats, but no many prettier cages. When it is all over we find we have won a prize for the third prettiest cage. The child in us is delighted.

Divorced friends go by separately. It is the father's day to have the children. The children hold onto his hand and will not let it go to look closely at the cats. His shirt, the father's, is wrinkled. His hair is longer than it used to be. He is interested in breasts, mine, anyone's. His eyes drop at chest level and I am saddened for him because I do not have much for him to see.

At the end of the day, the cat-owner finalists believe we are all still here watching the last event out of avid interest. But they do not consider that we stay because we must stay until four o'clock, or we would not care which cat won. It is written in the application form. There is no going home until four o'clock.

A psychosomatic hair lingers in my throat for two days.

21.

Jackie's House: Being no one nowhere.

Jackie's House

You're angry because you don't like your face anymore. Or your hands. Or your clothes. You let him put you in the car, and you unroll the window for the usual last smile and kiss. It is routine. It is what you have in place of spontaneity anymore. You cannot stop going through the motions, because you would be accepting that it was nothing. You know it's nothing now, but you keep up the act because it is too frightening to think of what you would do with *nothing* after admitting it.

You have a pimple on your chin and it is a big one. It will be here to stay for awhile. You have new capillaries showing inside your thigh which are not temporary. They are marks of time and you resent being marked on when you have nothing to show for the time you've already spent.

As you drive away, you say, "I want to go somewhere, fly there, to the place where everything is happening. Like to Jackie's house."

22.

Flattery, second to men.

Flattery

All her life there have been men sitting around tables making drawings on papers and talking avidly about building something. And women always hushed, moving about on the periphery, bringing food and drink and hearing the talk and not understanding a word of it. And the lack of understanding breeding a respect. And The Women believing The Men were geniuses that had not yet risen.

And these women in her life had let the men take money (the only money) and spend it on their ideas (a do-dad machine of some sort) and they have believed along with the men that it was wonderful.

And now, in her own home, Phil and Alex sit on the floor while she and Mona creep past them, reverently. But she holds a private disgust and a humor for their automatic respect for the men. After awhile she does not contain it. She says, "For thousands, tens of thousands of years, women have listened to men in conference over *ideas*, and they have believed in them. We're conditioned. We've been taken. We're fools."

Phil smiles because he is visiting. And because he has had three gimlets. Alex swells up, ready to attack verbally but lets it out in a tired sigh. It would take too fine a verbal construction to put his wife in her place in front of their friends. He is not up to it. Finesse and tact are not part of ideas.

She goes away with Mona, to talk woman talk. And as they

talk, her mental fingers toy with Mona's thick eyebrows, so that later when Moan is gone, the eyebrows come back alone, and she wonders who they belong to.

For the rest of the evening she ignores the men and accepts tradition. She likes men, because once a man told her he thought she was honest because she didn't wear a bigger bra.

From the Bench

I sit at Disneyland and wait for everyone to finish having fun. A woman goes by with a pimple up her flower-petal sleeve. Little balls of Bird peck at popcorn everywhere. The boys who pass, hit the trash cans swinging doors. I am oily from the heat and I remember my oily face in the bathroom mirror. I looked like someone I didn't know. She was older than I thought and browner, tireder and less repairable.

All the clothes that pass are "mod." And all the bodies are not. A man takes a bit of a large phallic-shaped object from his wife. It must be a chocolate banana covered with nuts.

I sip a mint julep which I do not have a thirst for. And because it is sold at the snack stand it does not have liquor in it. The sun bears down on my right thigh. I see the woman pressing the banana into her husband's mouth again and his eyes grow half-mast and serious as he tries to nibble a piece loose, fighting the peanut coating.

Two thirty-eightish men act uninterested in me. I fight the If-they-only-knew-they-would-be syndrome and watch other people. An old man drinks coffee the way he must drink it every morning over in the valley in his wooden kitchen. He is raw-boned, lean and ruddy-faced, struggling to stay up-right. He is old. His wife wears a straw Western hat. I look away and remember that I am biased over everything because my mother has made me believe that people should be a certain way in each specific situation, and a certain way only, and all but those particular stereotypes are deviations, who are distinguishing.

I begin to wish my mint julep had liquor in it, not because I am unhappy but because it would take the edge off of boredom and confirm the senselessness that is there already.

A row of older people are looking like zoo creatures, as if they are peeling bananas, but they are tearing wrappers off of Kodak film. One of them calls it Kodiac film.

A heavy diamond ring goes by, on the hand of a man, giving him confidence. Without it he'd be an ordinary worker. There is the mark of Hard Hat set in his hair. He is with a woman who has such sides to her lips that when she chews her hot dog it is the way a caterpillar works on a leaf. People are twirling in cups and saucers off in the distance. And in America. Because this is where fantasy has come true. The great plastic saucers were born out of great molds somewhere.

Married men and single women send off the same signals. It is smugness. They have dealing power. Single men and married women are alike. They are lean of spirit, disillusioned and hurting. Or it comes to me that way as they pass. I send a hard boiled egg down my throat to my stomach and my stomach is bored with it.

I see a dried grape stem on the pavement where a sprinkler has been set. And because the water has deepened all the colors, pavement and stem, it is a thing of beauty and I want to press the stem in a frame. A man steps on it before I can go pick it up. All the feet in sandals belonging to men make me think of Jesus' feet. The white tendons, blue veins, the cleanness and the hairlessness of them.

Innocent little wives pass me. They are more innocent than the virgins because they are not valued any more. They go by with their stretch marks showing in the expressions on their faces. And they catch their husbands looking at young women. They shrug to protect themselves and they swallow and think of the new coiffure, the new dress, a tan, a diet, and the exercises they will read about. They think of all the means back to where they used to be, while the young virgins stroll by with wild eyes, soaking in the lack of competition and all the husbands' glances.

It's the hurt in the wives' eyes that give them their air of innocence. And the smugness in the virgins which give them their lack of it. The wives are broken animals. They have been humbled. The virgins remain rigid. They require things from the world yet because of their gifts. Because of their hymens they can make demands.

Disney would like to employ all beautiful girls. But there are not that many. Nature does not make that many. So he settles for youth. Because youth is a kind of beauty by itself.

Children pass by with their families or together with friends. And I remember about a child's love for a child. It is a love for what the other one is. The way they look and act. It does not enter into what they have yet. That will come later when they need something.

A father is crawling after his infant son on the grass, biting at his neck, making him squeal. A husband who looks as if he likes maximum efficiency is praising his wife who appears to be exhausted by making the preparations for her family to spend a day at Disneyland. People are laughing at an infant because it is doing all the things that they feel like doing in public, but can't.

A woman walks by awkwardly because she is lame. An infant walks by the same way because it is just learning to walk.

A crippled boy is asking the cashier at the snack stand why there's a picture of a crippled boy on a can for coins. There is hope in his eye that perhaps his kind has a place here at Disneyland.

A toddler is discovering the fine line that is drawn by his parents between the cuteness of the antics of his infant sister and of himself. His older sister hugs him to protect him from their parents. She hugs the baby in him, not the man. The man is not yet evident in the small boy. Later, when it becomes evident, she will not hug him.

All the waitresses from the snack stand rush to the window and look out on a newly planted flower garden to watch a gopher pulling greens down into his hole. When he appears, excitement runs through the uniformed women with their atrophied caps pinned to the backs of their puffed coifs. One says, "He's a big one," not because she knows sizes of gophers at all, but because it is what people say when their unaccustomed eyes see wildlife. And because they all want to believe they saw A BIG ONE.

An eight year old girl walks by alone, in between the bathroom and her waiting family, but pretending she is truly alone. And I remember when I was eight and had to take out the garbage. It was when I could pretend I was alone in the world and I used to imagine there was a camera on me and that I was in a movie. And that at the end of my life there would be a record of what I did, exactly as it was. That God and I could watch the movie of my time on earth. So I used to be careful about what I did.

And now I sit next to an old lady who has a hairy caterpillar for an upper lip and I wonder again if maybe it is that after all. If it is just the body positions we get in. That our life is made up of this and then that, walking, sitting, lying, climbing, and could be traced like a single snail trail, and at the end you examine the pattern and that's what it has been all about. Where you've been and the physical positions.

A rock group begins to play somewhere and because my body must know the sounds it makes inside itself, and the rock music imitates those sounds, it appeals to my guts. The rock music and my stomach begin to communicate automatically. And after awhile the rhythm makes me want to touch myself. The thought of touching myself insults a part of me though, because it immediately knows the difference. It knows that it would not be the hand of another person and it knows that it would be lonely afterward. Because it would not need a man and it wants to need a man, or someone besides itself.

Some couples walk by and the young lean animal is in them because they are in love. The fat slow dying animal is in the others who are not in love. With anything. A man. With life. Love is lean and strong. Not loving causes decay to emerge. I am thinking.

From as young as I can remember I was in love with a boy. Some boy somewhere. I remember that the feeling was as strong as it is now, as I listen to the music, and feel in love again, but with no one at all this time. I cannot stop thinking about love because the rock music is heavy with random sound which imitates random movement which is the sound and movement of the bed.

I wait on my bench, excited by the music, and wishing for any appetites at all. For thirst, for hunger, for something to satisfy. And I watch the roller coaster going down and remember how I felt destroyed, or on the way to being destroyed when I was on it earlier. All I could do was hang on as it went straight down. And although the track swooped up eventually and there was some elation, I doubted it on the way down. I could not see ahead past my fear and it looked down forever, as if I'd go down until I disappeared into blackness.

I watch the sun go down now, from my bench, and wait there, avoiding another ride and *fear*. And I wonder if that has come to take the place of *appetite*. Avoiding things that scare me.

23.

The Adjustment: Trying to feel something about aging.

The Adjustment

I never really was that pretty. Looking at old photographs I see that there wasn't that much to me. But it was the people back then. Everyone thought I was something. I could tell. They acted as if there was something about me. And I heard the word "pretty" a lot and saw them looking.

Daddy thought I was everything. He liked me a lot. I've never found another man to like me as much as he did. Or to need me as much.

My mother had a silent envy I think. It was little things, things she'd say and sometimes hostility. I looked like the kind of girl she had always wanted to be like at school when she was a girl. I was lean, blue-eyed and had a degree of knowing what was going on. She was heavy-set, giant breasted, built for an old world, a hungry world. And she was too poor to get in anywhere. I looked like my father. She married him because she wanted to get away from the dark heavy people, and into the blue-eyed ones. She called him a blonde even though he had black hair. She said people with fair skin and blue eyes were blonde.

When she found herself with a daughter who was what she had always wanted to be it was like holding all those school girls in her arms.

It made me feel superior in a lot of ways, her envy did. That, and my father's favoritism. All the rest of the kids turned out looking like my mother, dark, large. I was the only one who looked like him, and he liked his own looks better than hers, my mother's.

I had a dealing power then. I have never felt that kind of thing since. People have wanted me to do other things since then. They've wanted me to cover the food in the refrigerator properly and have gotten mad when I didn't. They have wanted me to drive the car more gently, and to concentrate on the instruction of how a camera works.

I try to tell myself that I never was that great after all, and to ignore the absence of what used to be there. I concentrate on getting the hose wound up in the yard just right, and keeping the things that are supposed to be organized in alphabetical order, arranged that way. But I miss the old credit I used to get for nothing. When I look in the mirror I look for what people used to see. And I try to make Alex say that I'm better than anyone else he's ever had.

24.

The Funeral: The dead one looked better than all in attendance.

The Funeral

Grandma had no right to be sitting there at Jesse's funeral. She was supposed to have been next and then Jesse and then Ruby and then my dad and so on according to age.

I sat in the back row and tried to feel sad about the way life was. The way it took people out of turn. I thought about Jesse, and how he had been here when I was born and how he had lasted all this time until now with his tight white head leaning back in his easy chair reading a Zane Grey novel. That was the only picture I had of him in my memory. My mother said he had been a lumberjack and a beautiful man when he was young, but I could only remember seeing him sitting in his chair with his eyes focused on the print of a Zane Grey paperback. I tired to imagine him walking around or sitting at the table or standing in the yard and I could not.

I read the pamphlet in my hand. It was about Jesse Leonard Lane, and when he was born and when he died and where he was from and where he lived most of the time. And I did not like seeing his life printed out on the green slip of paper as if it had been that easy. And a copy of it in each of our hands. I folded mine in half and put it in my purse, and sat back and watched the people over in the Friends section file in past the transparent curtain that separated relatives from friends.

And then I looked at the backs of his immediate family's heads. They were in the front row, with his wife in the first seat.

Next to her was her younger son Kenneth, who said he was going into the funeral business when he heard the total cost of his father's funeral, and his wife Putz, the German bride from twelve years before. Doris was next to her with her prematurely gray hair prepared and stiffened into a coif. The shape of a helmet. Beneath it was her sallow hatched face, and next to her was, Joe, her third husband. He was a big man who liked to drink extra rich milk, or pure cream, if he could get ahold of it, by turning the quart box up and swallowing over and over until it was empty. He had carbuncles on the back of his neck and I knew they were deposits of butterfat and I wondered why his doctor wouldn't tell him that. He would be next to die, falling like a great timber of a heart attack in a few years.

Beside him was Margie. She had come down from Oregon where she had lived for twenty-five years with a husband named Bill, who did not treat her right so he did not come to the funeral to let her family look at him. Margie sat hunched over because her bones were clutching together with arthritis, and pulling her with them. The secret everyone knew was that Bill had brought home a disease as a young husband and gave it to Margie and it had eventually caused the arthritis.

I could not take my eyes off the side of her face. Her eyes, (one would be removed in the not too far future from infection), were dry and sat deep inside dark hallows. Her teeth, only four left in front, were gray and decaying and had remained in position as her face fell back away from them over the years. She had come alone by Greyhound in her best clothes, a cotton print dress with rhinestone buttons and a cheap flat pair of black slip-on shoes. Everyone knew she had gotten a rotten deal out of life. But only I knew the reason why. It was because she had started running around too young. My mother had told me long ago the story of Margie and her wild boyfriends. There was a photograph of a fat-cheeked rosy-faced girl with a lovely body standing by the front porch, with a slouching boyfriend. It was Margie and Bill. Jesse had tried to be strict but Ruby couldn't bear to let her daughter miss all the fun.

It was a horror story that would scar any young girl into remaining a good girl for awhile. And I did. For twenty-three years.

I wondered what Jesse would have done back then, in his chair, if he could have seen his daughter coming to his funeral as she looked now. I wondered if he would have put down his novels and tried everything or anything to prevent it, if he would have just a glimpse of foresight.

I could not go past Margie for awhile. I had heard that her oldest son had broken a track record and was sent off to college on a scholarship. And her oldest daughter had run off and gotten married at sixteen and the other two children were still in school wearing the new watches Ruby had sent them from money she earned working as a nurse's aide in a hospital.

Ruby was not crying. Off to her left was the casket with Jesse in it, laying on his back with his hands folded. I knew ruby would rather cry about Margie than Jessie. And I knew Margie regarded her father's death as a minor tragedy compared to what she'd been through and there would be no tears over it.

Next to Margie was Bob her brother, the oldest of the children, who had pulled a scab off his sore big toe and got gangrene in it and almost died. He leaned against his wife and together they could not stop crying. Lola blew her nose and wiped her eyes and leaned against bob and offered him her handkerchief. It was silent weeping. And I believe Lola cried for all the wretchedness in her entire life and because Bob was about to die any time of diabetes, and did soon enough, and because she could hardly walk due to a bad back. She had been in a car accident, first and then beaten by her first husband. And my mother said Bob had eaten too much white bread all his life and would not stop and that's why he went into insulin chock regularly.

Some singing started. I could tell right away they were from the Church of Christ. A woman sang bass and there old male voices came out harmonizing the melody. They sang about meeting by the river someday. My mother's plump hands kept fidgeting. She held a hankie. Her thumbs twitched over an embroidered bump and she sighed. I knew she would not shed a tear over Jesse because she had told him long ago he should be eating brown bread instead of white and green leafy vegetables instead of starchy potatoes and gravy. She knew this would happen some day, that he would die of something.

When she began to cry I knew it was because she remembered her second husband's funeral.

I sat there and wondered why I couldn't feel anything. I had known Jesse all of my life.

25.

The Time in Between: more public pathos, feeling sorry for the whole human race, herself included.

The Time in Between

She leaves her car and walks toward the stationery story where she knows lay the notebooks she likes. They are the right kind, with narrow lines and thick, packed full of pages and shen she holds one in her hand she wants to write in it. She has filled the old one and now makes her way to buy a new one.

A half man comes out of See's Candies on his wheel board, fighting the ridge where the sidewalk connects with the store floor tile, and she wants to ask him if she can give him a pull, but looks away instead because it is not nice to look at his struggle. He had been cut in half once, just below his genitals and fastened to a board in order to be able to go out and shop. He holds a bag of candy which is about to scrape the ground, but he holds it up an inch higher and rolls over the hump and makes his way down the sidewalk.

As she passes Thrifty, she sees a young blonde couple who are in love because the girl puts her hand on the man's shoulder while she waits for him to open the car door. She wears a big red bra under a white blouse and she has lean hips, the same width as his. They are wearing identical pants.

An old man and woman make their way to the automatic door, walking as if there are large rocks in their paths. She pictures them in bed and she knows that no matter what they do they cannot love with the freeness and the joy of the young blondes. Their minds are on prescriptions and when to talke them and what if they forget to. She sees their old and stiff bodies full of medicine and watches to detect if there is any chance for an easy carefree love to come from them when the veins stand out big and the blotched bony hands and the necks are like the loose necks of turtles and the eyes are growing cataracts and thre is no telling how the bowels are.

The young blondes pass her in their Volkswagen on their way to go to bed again with ease, unaware of their smooth silkiness which exists without their asking.

She enters Banks stationery store and heads for the notebooks she likes. There is a neat stack of them. She takes one and looks at the price even though she knows it will say sixtynine cents. She wants to see how the person who stocked the shelves wrote it this time, with his grease pencil. As she pays for it she pictures herself kicking and thrashing on a white sheet somewhere, and a doctor speaking softly to her that he's sorry and everyone is sorry and he knows what she means, but they must all grow old and one must accept it. And the more she whines and cries, the more he sympathizes until she takes it too far and then he grows impatient and goes off angry with her and glad that she is suffering from growing old. He has his satisfaction without having to do anything to shut her up, in just knowing she cannot accept it.

As she leaves the store she peels the bag off her new notebook and wads it up with the sales slip and drops them in a trash bin. She carries her notebook naked and feels its thick paper cover. It is a good feeling and she knows it will be awhile yet before she's that old. But it has been awhile, too, since she was that young.

*I shout, "No, you can't go with me," to all the children in the world.
I shake them off my shoulders and brush them loose from my hands
and feet and go to a coffee shop by myself. And order a single cup of
coffee. No sugars. Nothing that will spill or drip. And I sit alone on
a single stool. Very still. Motionless. And once in awhile I lift the
single cup to my mouth and pour in some of the dark brown fluid.
I do this for a long time. Over and over until it becomes one time.
One movement. While people I do not know come and go. I do not
need to look at them because I do not know them. I do not owe them
words or a turn of my head to show them I am friendly when I am
not. My elbow is the only bendible place in me. I sit rigid and my
elbow allows the cup to come and go. I sip and inhale in unison
and my eyes stay in one place. They see all that they want to see
of movement from their peripheral abilities. Inside me I see all the
women I came from, moving about all their lives, bustling, never
getting to or wanting to sit still enough to feel the movement of the
earth as it spins. Always being the movement themselves. Moving
their hands over cloth and food and dirt and flesh. Moving their
bodies under men and over territories. Moving their eyes and mouths.
Unceasingly. And I cannot be still enough. While movement soaks
in to me from all sides. From everywhere. I hold still for all of them.
For everyone. I cannot hold still enough. For long enough. I cannot
return to the source of all the stillness there is. Not still enough to see
movement anew. And to know it. To see it. The movement I must
see. Before I have to move again.*

26.

The Awakening

Jeannie had just awakened from a nap. She felt a calm possessing her. The house was quiet. A sense of control came over her. She did not move, and her body held a still deep warmth that she did not want to disturb. Slowly she pushed the cover off her and felt the coldness of the room. She got up without a sound and listened to the soundless rooms as she made her way to the bathroom. It was not the house she had lay down in. That had been full of loud children and cats, the radio, and the toilet running.

Jeannie did not want to break the silence. She had gone far away from the self she had been before the nap. She was somewhere else, maybe inside at the center of control. She thought, I will water the garden now and then that will be done. Each day I will water it. I will never forget, and the corn will grow. She went out, turned on the hose, pressed her thumb over the end of it and listened to the sound of water coming through the coils until it spurted out the end. Her thumb rode on the spray and played the water into patterns which fell in a broad curve of rain drops on the brown furrows of soil. On top of each mound was a green row of new plants. It was four p.m. The sun broke from beneath clouds that were too high to hide it. Bright yellow touched Jeannie's garden and warmed her back and she looked at the sky and watched the swallows diving and careening. She remembered that she used to think the swallows loved to do that, but later she learned they were driven to do it. With the thought of instinct, Jeannie felt a twinge of anger over that.

She thought of people who were not standing and spraying their gardens and watching the swallows, and the anger stayed. She looked away from the swallows because she began not liking them now. She looked at the trees and saw the way they were stuck into the ground. They had a root system which would not let them go. She felt the tightness of it holding them.

The yellow sun had disappeared and gray came in its place, and Jeannie turned and shaded her eyes and looked for the sun. It was behind a cabbage-shaped cloud. The air was clear because of the wind. She saw the mountains behind her house standing out dark blue. They were bold and pressing big upon her where before they had stood back behind mist. A pigeon landed on a telephone pole and watched her, leaning it's head awkwardly. It was alone. Goosebumps broke out on her arms. She tiptoed through the wet grass and touched her naked ankles and rolled down to her bare feet. She shivered and she knew that if she threw a handful of bread crusts on her garden the pigeons would eat them. That inside its craw there was still room for a feast. But she would not throw bread crusts and it would sleep that night without them. It would not be hungry and it would not be full. And it would go on living.

She went inside the house and pulled the door shut fast before it could squeak and wake the children. Knowing they were getting sleep fed a need in her. It made her feel competent. She thought, I am a good mother. I watered the corn so that it is growing and I give my children sleep so that they are growing. We are safe. I am safe. She turned on the heater and shut all the windows. The heat poured out as the fan went on, and Jeannie felt intelligent. I closed all the windows. I will always close all the windows. I will never let the heat from the heater be pulled outside through an open window to be wasted. Jeannie felt the control staying with her. Her breathing deepened and she sat in a chair and listened to the silence of the home which she had created. The silence that meant she had organized her life so that nothing wild was running through it. No doors were banging, nothing was burning on the stove. There was only the quiet bubbling of the lima beans from the kitchen.

She watched the green trees waving in the wind outside

from her front window. She wished they were free. They only appeared to be. She saw the birds settle on the telephone wire and then fly off to find a tree. She wished the birds were free. The pupils of her eyes narrowed as the bright yellow from the sun, still sinking lower than the clouds, flooded things again before the dark came. She made up her mind that the children would eat the beans for dinner even though they didn't like them. She thought of the candy they had eaten over the weekend. She felt a touch of insecurity. Perhaps their teeth had developed some cavities and their tissues had been deprived of nutrients. She was afraid that she had allowed something in them to be destroyed. Fear came over her and she worried about them. She began to wish for something she did not know a word for. It was a want and the want became a thing pressing inside of her head. Her head began to ache.

The day was going. It was being wiped away by long sweeps of shadow. Jeannie was afraid for the outside to be dark and to know that she would not be able to see. She wanted to see everywhere to make sure that she and her children were safe. She listened to the beans bubbling on the stove. The smell came to her. She heard one of her children getting up from bed. Karen walked into the room and searched for her mother. She sees Jeannie in the chair. The stillness was broken. The silence was filled with Karen's movement as she walked to Jeannie and sat down and waited for her to put her arm around her and pat her for waking up. Jeannie points to the swallows and says, "See, they are catching insects." She did not tell her anything more. Karen said she wanted to go see the kittens, and she got up and walked away from her and went back to her bedroom where, in a box, a mother cat lay with blood on the fur around her bottom and four white kittens nursing.

Jeannie was saddened as Karen left her. The outdoors had turned dark. She felt the want for something pushing on the inside of her forehead. It came on strong and she wondered if she wanted it to be daylight forever and to never get dark.

27.

Forces

There are two forces. Pulling at her. That she knows of. Has identified. One is made up of things called jogging, reading, etc. the other is packed with things called drinking, smoking, etc. She is constantly tugged, having no self outside their demands. Subject to their poles of gravitation.

Early in the morning, in the time after sleep and before wake, there is a pureness when the jogging and reading one sneaks to her and whispers *be good*. Be pure and good. And she is. She believes she is. But as the day increases in complications, as involvement rolls her around and lays her out vulnerable, the drinking and smoking one comes boldly to beckon her: *Go away with me.*

In girlhood she did not know the names of the forces. She used to call herself by their names. *Good. Bad.* She was *bad* when a boy kissed her. She was *good* after she punished herself with long therapeutic sessions at the ironing board. The forces were hidden then. Inside her. And she did not separate herself from them. Later they rose up and stood blatantly independent, making it demonstrative that they were using her. As a battle field. And that she was only a witness. To their conflict.

She wanted peace. When they came she did not know if she were being chased or lured. But they always took her to a place called *away*.

At a meeting of people she sees a woman's back. The woman is her age. The back has gone soft under polyester coverings. Brassiere straps dig into flesh and leave paths. A bulge rests along the waist. She is not old. She is not young. This woman curls her dark blonde hair in a Fifties style.

At the meeting of people, where they listen to a lecture, she sees an old woman's thumb. It dips in at the first joint where it should jut out. Arthritis. The woman claps when the lecture is over and her eyes go to the deformed thumb to watch the way deformity applauds.

At the meeting she sees the tight kinky head of a husband who is the same age as his father-in-law. The father-in-law who sits beside him and lets the granddaughter jump up and down in her stocking feet on his fifty-five year old legs, because it is the first touching he's had since his wife stopped bothering. A new female has focused on him, rubbing his old cheeks, patting his hair. His face responds as if he is in love.

At this meeting there is a young mother with a stomach that has become a pouch not unlike a mother kangaroo's. Her young offspring sits on it as she comforts him with short arms. He pushes and rocks and the soft ample flesh folds and presses down over her upper thighs. And supports him.

She has just finished jogging. In fact she has jogged to the meeting. The audience sends sensations through her. She does not know if it is fear or joy. Horror and dread or fondness of the familiar.

There are two forces that will vie to separate, or let her believe she is separated, from the distorted back, ruptured stomach and deformed thumb. She will either jog and read or drink and eat in response. It is the effect of the forces. She will not be able to vary the reaction and combine some from the jog side with the eating side. She cannot combine read with drink. They do not mix. She has tried it. For balance. To balance the forces and steady them.

Earlier in the day, a boy who grew up drove by in his car with its rear-end up in the air and loud pipes sounding out. He flew by her as she jogged along the street, and she saw an incredulous look in his face. *What the... is she still jogging... What's her trip.* She had been jogging when he didn't know what was going on; when he was selling seeds and Christmas cards in order to earn money for a bike. He thought she was a phase in his life, that her jogging belonged to that period in his life and would pass. He left town for awhile and came back a grown man in a car, going fast, making noise. He saw her as an apparition still making its way along the tarred shoulder of the road. His eyes said, *What for? What in the hell is she running so much for. Where is she going.* He looked as if he had just seen the old bicycle he outgrew.

She was dated by his glance. She saw herself as a little old lady in tennis shoes from Pasadena still running along the road. And still not knowing if she was running away from something or toward it. But knowing that she must run. Or she must read. Or she must over eat. Or she must drink. Because the forces come and a battle ensues and one always wins and takes her to a place called *Away*.

28.

Decision

I sit next to a young man. But I am wise. Five years before I was not wise. I sat next to a young man and turned and said, "Hi." I know where it can go. He will turn. He will like my face and my manner. The way I am not sure of anything. And the imperfection of my face. He will want to help me to be sure of things. And to like the imperfections. Through this approach I will learn of his sureness and his doubts. Of what he likes and doesn't like. Wants and has never wanted. Wishes for and does not wish for. I will learn the size of his dick and of his wallet. The size of his heart and the extent of his generosity and of his greed. His need to love and his inability to love. Of the source of his quirks and perversions.

I do not turn and say, "Hi." We do not eventually touch hands, touch mouths, roll around in a front seat, in a bed, on a couch, break an aluminum lawn chair from the weight of our passion. We do not sit on a lawn, at the beach in the sand. Everywhere, anywhere, using places and positions and movements as a medium to find out all there is to know about him and more than I want to know. And to imprint things I will want not to remember later, but cannot forget.

I see the lean youngness of his arms and the big joints of his knees and elbows. The same leanness and bigness that sat there before, five years ago and now lies rotting in a grave. I do not turn. There would be no sense to it. It would be repetition, a new set of details. Learning that there is a mother somewhere that he's devoted to or not devoted to. An early childhood training that he reacts against there inside his head. That he functions from a reward and punishment conditioning and that he suffers because of his place in the family. Some family somewhere that I would learn about. I would learn of his experiences: if not in the Peace Corps in Bolivia, then a summer in San Diego or a winter at Tahoe where he became *aware* of something, of himself, his limitations or talents, that interfere now. His value through some female.

It would be the same but different. I grow tired, sad, sitting next to him. Disgusted that it would be the same with different names and places and trivia. The dialogue being written for us years ago. For male and female. That this is all we would be able to say to each other. The intrigue, the calling or not calling, the showing-up or not showing-up, and eventually the name-calling being routine.

I do not turn.

29.

Beverly

I saw Beverly today, talking along Milpas. She went into the bank. Business must be good. She is a whore. For black men. She has no teeth and sparse stringy hair, a hump on her back and large pale green eyes. She is skinny. And she is my age. I went to school with her. In the seventh grade she told me a secret, that Slim, her uncle "did things" to her on the front porch "where even God could see."

I look around at her in the bank and smile. She smiles back, wondering why I'm looking. She does not remember me. I want to go to her and tell her everything I remember about us as school girls. I want to know what she remembers about us. And about me. I want to know how we are recorded in each other's minds. How am I in her mind now. I want her to know how she is in mine. I want to ask her if she remembers a little girl in seventh grade who was shy and quiet and always wore boys pants with a yellow old plaid coat. Who had crooked braids and a longish nose and freckles. Who used to listen to her secrets and side with her against Mrs. Carmichael. And if she says *yes*, I'll exclaim, "*That was me!*"

She will look and see me *grown up* and be envious that I grew up so well, came out of childhood, the awkwardness and dirtiness and sticky-fingeredness of childhood, into adulthood clean and unscathed. And *safe*.

She would see that there is lots of stuff between me and destruction *now*, unlike her. She would have only to look at my husband writing out a deposit slip, to detect the amount of safety I have acquired in our same length of time on the same earth. And the thick useless soles on the ends of my feet. Fun shoes. Fun clothes. All easy and fun things on *me*. Better than childhood when she and I were both talking on the playground threadbare. And now she stands there without the only wealth she ever had, *her youth*. In serious clothes. Clothes to hide her, not to display her. Clothes to keep her covered and protected. Cotton dark clothes drooping on her caved-in frame, laying over the hump on her back, hanging over her frail bruised, hairy, veined, knobbed legs. Legs that open for black men because white men don't want her. Because they know about white legs like that. While black men just must see *white*. There are no fine lines. No good or bad or medium. No capacity to discriminate outside of *black*. Or why do they want her?

I want to go to Beverly and help her. I want to say, "See, I have a lot of stuff now. I'm better off than you are and I *knew* I would be way back then in seventh grade. I knew nothing would turn out for you because of the way you said, 'even God could see what your uncle did on the front porch... '"

I want to hear her tell me that I turned out better than she did so her mind will be ready to accept my teaching. And then I will discuss why. I will reform her. I will get a tightness in my throat and tears in my eyes and save her. I will say, "Eat oranges and jog... Put live flowers in vases all over the inside of your house. Bring *nature* in. Bring the *outdoors* in. Open all the windows. Let fresh air in. Throw away anything plastic that collects dust. Turn your bed inside out and let the sun kill the germs. Go to the beach and cook your poor infected, bruised pale dying flesh in the sunshine and bathe it in the surf. And cure it. *Live with a swish*. And don't sell sex anymore. Give it away out of the kindness of your heart and for *pleasure*. Don't be a whore. I don't want you to be. I don't want you to have gone so far away from the girls we used to be and the plans we made... "

And I want her to be able to tell me, "Oh, M.. I understand why my uncle violated me. And I know what I'm doing. I know why I'm caught. I know my health is gone. I know all that I am.

I know the girl I used to be. I haven't forgotten the promises she made to the lady I would be some day. I am conscious of the transition from her to *this*. I know I have a humped back because I never threw my shoulders back. Because I had no lust, no exuberance...."

But I do not turn around and look at Beverly again. It would be rude. She would think I was staring because she is a sight. She may cringe and feel wretched all day if I *gawk* in her direction again. And if I should go over and get her to remember us, there in the bank, she would wonder why I bothered. It is finished. Our pasts. Why belabor them. She will suspect pity. Or that I want to compare us and gloat. She will eventually resent it being pointed out. That *I made it and she didn't*. Or she will simply tolerate my friendliness, weary, and knowing I feel beautiful because of her wretchedness. That I would not go up to a fellow student who had become famous and say, "Hi, let's compare notes."

Beverly speaks with the teller behind the loans counter. I leave with my husband who is a *trophy* in Beverly's eyes. And I know it will be a long time before I bump into her again. I will talk to her next time. Something must be said. Before we die. She must know what is in my heart. I must know what is in my heart. I must go to her next time in order to find out what is in my heart.

30.

A Dislocated Eye

We want excitement. There is a dark and wretched bar, pool, hamburger, beer place two miles up the street. They also have a cigarette machine for Alex. So we jump in the car. There are pick-up trucks parked in front and dusty older cars. I am already excited. It is better than doing dishes. We will be able to sit back or lean forward. On our elbows. It will be time out and maybe something will happen that doesn't happen at home. So we go in and it's as if we swagger and have hair in the pits of our arms that smells of construction worker sweat.

We take a table alongside the cinder block wall, letting our eyes adjust to the dark. There are three Mexicans around the pool table in the back, shuffling on the wooden floor with their work boots, as they teach their two small sons how to play. One, an uncle, sits at a table picking up French fries and stuffing them into his mouth one after another as if he is really hungry. He has large white teeth. I think of him eating beans. They drink beer from dark bottles. The jukebox is playing "The First Time Ever I Saw Your Face" over and over again and then changes to "Killing Me Softly." It is being pumped by a long-legged Italian in white polyester pants and a nylon body shirt in purples and grays. The grays are the same multi-shades as his curly full head of rich shiny Italian hair. He stands at the bar between two stools when he is not striding across to the jukebox. A soft belly pushes gently at his shirt. He never looks at me, not even when I enter which strikes me as unusual. I detect loyalty to another woman in him. A woman he is remembering as he plays Roberta Flack over and over.

We order beers and Alex goes over and punches buttons on the cigarette machine and returns without looking at anything or anyone. He is a very proper man who told me in the beginning that I should not stare at people the way I do, not because they would care, but because people I am not aware of will be seeing me looking at these people and will think there is something strange about me. That only children can get away with that kind of scrutiny without making everyone nervous. So I became less obvious. I sit with my back pressed on the cinder block wall, sideways in my chair, and lift the glass of beer and take in the Mexicans and the Italian without looking at them in a way they would notice.

Two dusty young men with dry blonde curls and Hawaiian rayon shirts hunch over the bar drinking beer and eating hamburgers. There is nothing of interest about them. They are not good-looking. Only their style evokes excitement. They have glanced up only when we came in and then resumed their interest in the plates beneath their faces. There was nothing of interest in us to them. We wait. We are all waiting for something.

Perhaps we are waiting for someone to come in who will be the person we have always been waiting for. Someone to excite us. Someone extraordinary, even weird. Maybe a freak or the strangest character we can imagine. Someone with a dislocated eye, or wearing a gun. Someone with his fly open and his private place exposed. A cripple or a criminal, or a monster in human form. Someone who has already freed himself from the ties that hold the rest of us. Someone who has already broken out of the mold. For us. Someone who is living our wildest dreams. Someone who will make us live or cause us to die but will not allow us to be in between.

The Italian is restless. He cannot sit down. His eyes go to the door as if he is a dog waiting for a dead master. His knees lock and he leans against the bar and swivels on his heels to reach the bottle of beer which he pours to keep his glass full. His eyes wander and pace. He gazes and gazes and cannot gaze enough. When he turns and watches the Mexicans with their sons, a smile creeps into the corners of his thin Italian mouth and his dark watery eyes go funny, as if he is making room in his heart for *love of little children and fathers*. As if he is seeing a sweet, sweet hearth scene. As if he is not in a bar watching a family bend over a pool table. As if he sees more than that. Or through it or into it. His lips move and I see, without making it apparent that I am seeing him, that he talks to himself.

One of the Mexicans has caught his smile and returns it. He comes up to get another bottle of beer, and the Italian opens a conversation with a question. I do not catch the question because I am trying to pretend I am not listening. The Mexican begins with an explanation, a condescension, which defies his appearance. I thought he would be rough. On equal standing. His voice is high and has a tone of apology as he defers to the Italian. He begins with "Me likes...." And goes on in broken English and hand movements and grins. I do not like seeing it so I turn and face the screen door and give him his privacy.

Suddenly the door opens and our eyes squint and hurt with the glare as we make out a very beautiful Mexican girl. She hesitates a moment in the bright light and then enters letting the door close without a sound. She is the kind you would call Spanish out of respect. She is wearing a very wide radiant smile, bright eyes, and a white monks cloth blouse with long flowing virgin sleeves covered with rustic lace. And dark glasses perched in her hair. Thin new jeans and cork platforms. She enters as if onto a stage where her role is about to begin. A prima donna. The Italian has turned from his vigilance of the door just seconds before to speak to the Mexican. She hurries past, even smiling at me, the competition, confident, proud, radiant. I respond, taken by the performance, and smile back. She goes quickly, surreptitiously on small feet without a sound, involved in her private very personal dance into the depths of the room and on to the Italian and touches him with long polished fingernails. It is his cue. He turns immediately, ready, knowing the touch and his arms are around her. They are together. And we know something. Something important about them. And about ourselves. It is what we came for.

Alex has not seen because it is not proper to stare at people. He has missed the drama. She finishes a phrase in Spanish to the Mexican who laughs and politely wanders to the back of the room. I try not to notice her upside-down valentine ass as she slides up onto a high stool beside her man. I try not to see her small waist bound with a monks cloth sash and the strong lean back muscles like two young snakes crawling along each side of her spine. I try not to watch the way his hand finds and feels these muscles and rubs them over and over with clean Italian fingers. And the way his index finger will one day be the kind that turns in at the last joint with arthritis when he's old and decrepit. It has a hint of its future journey now as he pets her strong Spanish back. The lace on her sleeves lays all over the counter as she leans and gazes into his lips that mumble words to her. Words I cannot hear but already know. I see the way she has ratted her hair for the occasion and her thin weak female arms that have the potential for sudsing out his gray and purple nylon body suit one day.

Alex sighs out through the nostrils, blowing smoke, bored, wanting to get back to the work we have left waiting for us even though it is a lifetime of work. He has not given up hope of finishing it in just one more day, one more week, one more month, or maybe one more good year. And then we can begin our real lives. After we finish the work that needs to be done, then there will be time for beautiful people to come to us and wake us up and give us life. To make us know the work is over and the living has begun.

We leave. I am excited. He still waits for excitement.